D1327424

CHAIM WALDER

People talk about...themselves!

TRANSLATED BY CHAVA WILSCHANSKI

FELDHEIM PUBLISHERS
JERUSALEM   NEW YORK

Adapted from the Hebrew, *Anashim Mesaprim al Atzmam*

First published 2002

ISBN 1-58330-510-6

Copyright © 2002 by Chaim Walder

FELDHEIM PUBLISHERS
POB 35002 / Jerusalem, Israel

www.feldheim.com

10   9   8

Printed in Israel

To my dear father הי״ו:

Whose image, clarity of vision, and words
are reflected in every one of
my stories and articles.

"For my soul is bound up in his"

Abba —

To each of your children you give
from your heart, from your wisdom,
from your resources,
and from your own unique personality.

But most of all, you give...yourself.

Other Books in English by the Author

Kids Speak
More Kids Speak
Kids Speak 3
Kids Speak 4
Our Heroes
That's Me, Tzviki Green
Listen to the Soul
Subject to Change

From the Author

D
ear Reader,
   Truth is stranger than fiction. The destruction of the Twin Towers of the World Trade Center in New York shows us that we can experience events so unbelievable that no writer could have invented them.

The stories in these pages are true, written by real people about their own lives. The letters are taken from the many sent to me over the course of a number of years. Although my post office box was originally intended for children's letters [for the Kids Speak series], eventually half of my mail was from adults.

I have learned that people don't want to keep their stories to themselves, that they are looking for someone to tell their story to, someone who will respond with understanding and sympathy. I feel privileged that they honored me with that role.

Sometimes these personal stories came in the form of long letters, sometimes in a few short lines that were expanded after a conversation in my office. In some cases I had to change elements in the story in order to protect the writer's privacy, even switching masculine and feminine genders when necessary. I also put some of the stories into words that would convey the writer's message more accurately. Other stories are virtually unchanged. But whether they were altered or appear verbatim, each and every one reflects a true life experience, experience that all of us can learn and benefit from.

I would like to express my thanks to the following:

First and foremost, the hundreds of people who have entrusted me with their most personal stories, knowing that they may be published;

Radio station *Kol HaNeshamah*, that broadcast the stories and as a result brought many more;

To the devoted staff of *Kol HaNeshamah* who give their all to spread Torah and *Yiddishkeit*, in particular Rabbi Yehudah Ronen, Ave Segal, Motti ben David, and David Sinai;

And finally, to the listening audience of thousands in Israel and all over the world who tune in to my program and respond with warmth and interest.

May God grant that all the obstacles and deceit that weigh on people's hearts be removed, and may this book be another step on the way to enabling people to speak about themselves.

Chaim Walder
Cheshvan 5762
November 2001

Contents

The Scar

Dear Rabbi Walder,

I've noticed that the letters you read from listeners often deal with the surprising twists and turns of life, and how simple things lead to unexpected events. This is why I have decided to write my story to you. If it weren't true, it would seem impossible!

When I was nine years old, my family spent the week of Sukkos at a beautiful, rural resort in the Galilee which catered to religious families. One day during *Chol HaMo'ed*, I took my little sister out for a walk in her stroller. We went along one of the many tree-lined paths, and stopped to sit under a tall tree, where I played with her and I told her a story.

I hadn't realized how far we had walked from the center of the resort until suddenly a group of children appeared. I could tell they weren't from the families staying at the resort — maybe they came from a neighboring village. They were wild, noisy children who seemed to want to make trouble, and they frightened me. As they ran toward me, yelling, I quickly climbed into the tree, but then I realized they might scare my little sister sitting in her stroller. Before I could climb down, however, the gang had arrived. They surrounded the tree and started to shake its branches. It was not a strong tree, and I swung wildly from side to side, screaming with fear and begging them to stop. I thought my life was in danger, but they were having a great time. When my little sister saw me screaming, she started screaming too, and this only made them wilder. I held onto the branches for dear life.

And then he came. A religious boy, around 12 or 13 years old, came running towards the gang, shouting at them to stop. One of them hit him and said, "Get lost and mind your own business!" I called out to him to go and get help. They were shaking the branches wildly, and I heard one of them say, "She can't last up there forever, in the end she'll fall down."

But my rescuer saw my terror and decided to act — he kicked them in the shins, grabbed at their shirts, and hit them. They hit him back, very hard, but he would not stop. Suddenly one of them yelled, "Now you're in big trouble!" and the whole gang set upon him. As he started to run away, with all of them after him, he signaled to me to get down from the tree. They caught up with him, grabbed him, and began hitting him with a beam of wood. I quickly scrambled down the tree, took my sister, and ran as fast as I could.

Once back in the center of the resort, I cried out for help, and several people set off towards the trees. They returned a few minutes later carrying my savior —who was covered in blood. I tried to get closer, but my mother took me into our rooms to calm me down.

I didn't leave our rooms till the following day. I tried to find out what had happened to the boy — I was afraid they had killed him! But my parents assured me that he had been taken to the hospital, and he wasn't badly hurt. I always wondered, though, if my father had told me the whole truth.

As I grew older, I felt I had to know what had happened to the boy who had saved me. My parents called the people who ran the resort (which had since closed down), but they didn't know anything about it.

Many years passed. I could not forget — the incident remained engraved in my heart.

When I turned 19, I began to receive suggestions for *shidduchim*. I started to date, but it was not smooth sailing. People began to say that I was too choosy, that maybe I didn't really want to get married — which wasn't true at all. When I was 23, someone suggested a young man named Yehudah. We made inquiries about him and heard only favorable reports. I wondered why he was not married yet (he was already 26 years old).

I agreed to meet him.

When I met him, I understood why he was still single. After one meeting, I saw that he was a really special person, in fact the most suitable young man I had ever met — intelligent, kind, with a fine character, and very learned in Torah. In short, he had everything. He was also tall and handsome — except for one thing. His face was marked by a terrible, deep scar that ran from his eye to his chin. It was shocking — a kind, gentle face ruined by this awful scar. It was difficult to look at him.

I told the matchmaker that I was not interested in continuing, but she, as well as my parents, tried to convince me otherwise. They told me to try to meet Yehudah again and maybe I would get used to him. Since I was really taken with his personality, I went out with him several more times — but the scar always came between us. (This had happened to him countless times before, he told me later. Things would start out well but because of that horrifying scar, no girl would continue to date him.)

On our fifth date (no other girl had lasted that long) he told me that he felt I was the right partner for him, and he tried to find out how I felt about it.

I tried to avoid giving a straight answer. I said "Well, you're a wonderful person, but...." I didn't know how to put into words what I felt, but I must have been staring at the scar as I spoke.

"You don't have to continue with the 'but...,'" he replied. "I know what you mean. If you haven't managed to overlook the scar by now, I guess you'll never come to terms with it."

I remained silent, not knowing what to reply.

He suggested that I go home and think seriously about whether I could ever get used to his scar. We started walking towards a cab.

I was so embarrassed, I did not know what to say. Then — I don't know why, maybe I just had to find something to talk about — I asked how he got the scar.

Yehudah smiled sadly. "I'll tell you the story," he began, "but I'm sure you won't think highly of me because of it! It happened when I was 12 years old... a gang of boys hit me with a beam of wood. Unfortunately, a nail was sticking out of it, and it tore open my face." He stopped, clearly upset at the memory. "I really don't know why I'm telling you this. You probably think I was a wild kid who loved a fight!"

Everything was spinning around me. "Wh...where did this happen?" I managed to stammer.

"My aunt and uncle were staying at a certain resort during Sukkos, and my family went to visit them. A gang of wild kids had started bothering a little girl in the woods. I was simply trying to help her, but they attacked me viciously." He smiled sadly, and I saw that tears filled his eyes. "And that's the story. Over the years, I had managed to forget the whole thing but once I started going on *shidduchim* it all came back to me. For the last five years I've been dating — and it seems that Hashem is making sure that every day I remember the story."

I began to tremble, and then burst into tears. He didn't know what to do! We sat down on a bench and in between sobs, I managed to blurt out that I was the girl he had saved.

Yehudah was dumbfounded, and at the beginning he even wondered if I was telling the truth. When I filled him in on more details, he realized that it was really me!

My joy was indescribable. In one split second all my doubts about him vanished into thin air. The very scar which had led me to reject this man now caused me to answer yes to his marriage proposal! That night we agreed to become engaged. We are now married, Rabbi Walder, and, as the saying goes, we are living happily ever after.

Rabbi Walder, my tears are flowing as I write this letter to you. No one except my immediate family knows my wonderful story. You often read sad letters on your program, but I am sure you will be happy to read my happy one!

Nothing happens by chance. Hashem is in charge of everything, and every day I thank Him for my wonderful husband, and for the amazing way that He brought us together.

It might surprise you, Rabbi Walder, but I offer my greatest thanks to Hashem for my husband's scar. The scar is what kept him waiting all those years — waiting for me! I think I understand all those girls who would not marry him because of the scar. After all, it meant nothing to them — it was *my* scar.

Forgive Me

Dear Rabbi Walder,
My story is a long and sad one. My husband and I were blessed with seven wonderful children and we are — or were — an exemplary family. Our oldest daughter, Rivka, was the pride of our family. She was beautiful and smart — the smartest girl in her class. Not only was she a conscientious student herself, but she was a good friend too, and spent hours with her classmates helping them with their homework. She was a wonderful help in the house, and was always willing to take care of the younger children. She and I were great friends. She was so trustworthy that if she needed money for anything, she would simply have to tell me, and I would give her the money, no questions asked. In return for our boundless trust, Rivka gave us boundless *nachas*. In our eyes she was perfect.

Two months before Rivka's eighteenth birthday, an acquaintance phoned me and told me in vague terms to "take a good look at what's going on with your daughter Rivka." I was puzzled and also insulted by the call. When I mentioned this to Rivka, she looked a little flustered but said that probably some jealous person just wanted to spread some gossip.

Over the next few weeks, there were certain indications that not all was as it should be, but at the time we didn't really pay attention. Rivka's good friends stopped coming over, and some of them even dropped hints that Rivka was going through a difficult time — but we ignored this, as it made no sense to us. We thought perhaps the girls had quarreled or something like that.

We had no idea that our world was about to fall apart.

In honor of Rivka's eighteenth birthday I bought her a gold necklace with a heart-shaped pendant studded with small diamonds. A very special and valuable gift for a special and valuable daughter, I told myself. I wrote her a long poem in which I expressed all my love for her. Tears of joy flowed freely as I wrote. Then I sat down to wait for her to come home from school.

I waited and waited but she never came.

At first I thought maybe she'd told me she'd be late and I'd forgotten, but as time passed we began to worry. We called her teacher, who told us that Rivka hadn't come to school at all that day! We began calling all her friends and slowly but surely, the terrible truth came out. It was too shocking to believe.

Our wonderful daughter had decided to get married without our permission or our knowledge. She had waited patiently until her eighteenth birthday, when she legally became of age and no longer needed our permission. She had gone alone to her *chuppah* at the local rabbinical council. She got married without her family and friends around her. Only the *chassan*'s side was present, and one of his relatives conducted the ceremony. Because she knew we would object to her husband, she had kept us out of the picture totally.

Life would never be the same again. Outwardly we carried on as usual — every morning we got up, davened, my husband went to work and our children went to school but they were fully aware that their parents were in deep distress and merely

7

"going through the motions." On the day that Rivka left, something died within us and we have not been able to rekindle the spark of life.

As you can imagine, we tried to fight our daughter's actions, but we learned that we had no legal recourse once our daughter reached the age of eighteen, the age of consent. I prefer not to describe her husband or his family. Suffice it to say that he had a shady past and came from an extremely problematic family.

I was devastated. Rivka contacted us and sent us messages, writing that she had run off like that only because she knew we would never accept her decision. How right she was! In addition to the pain, I was angry. I kept thinking: How dare she ruin our peaceful lives! Even if she had chosen to marry an honest man and a good Jew, what kind of girl decides to marry without her parents' blessing?

I turned to Hashem and I am ashamed to tell you what I prayed for, Rabbi Walder. I prayed that He punish Rivka for all the pain and sorrow she had caused our whole family. I begged Him *not* to grant her any happiness from her marriage because she had brought so much suffering to all of us. I admit that I was full of hatred, not love, for my own firstborn daughter.

Within the first three years of her marriage, Rivka gave birth to two children, but we still refused all contact with her. Our wounds were still open. The scandal caused us great difficulty in finding *shidduchim* for our other children. Because of her momentary whim, our entire family was ruined.

About two years ago we began to hear that all was not well in her marriage, that her husband beat her. Not only was I not sympathetic, but I even felt a slight vindication. The rumors continued to reach us, and with greater frequency. We heard that life was a daily struggle for her. She was penniless, had no support from friends or family, and had become essentially a slave at the mercy of a cruel husband. (We later discovered that the abuse had already begun in the first year of her marriage, but she was too proud to tell anyone at that time.)

We continued to ignore our daughter's existence until the day I was told that she had been admitted to the closed ward in a psychiatric hospital. That penetrated my wall of hatred, and I immediately dropped everything and rushed to her.

To see Rivka was to die all over again. My beautiful daughter was skin and bones. Her once beautiful eyes now stared vacantly into space. Her haggard face was expressionless.

Speechless, I sat at her bedside and just stared. This was Rivka? Tears of pain and bitterness, and regret, flowed down my cheeks.

We brought her two children to our home. Her husband and his family didn't want the burden of taking care of them.

I try to visit my daughter every day, and at her bedside I have begun to talk and talk. She does not always respond, but her condition has improved.

I feel terrible pangs of conscience about my role in this tragedy. Although I tried for years to repress my feelings, deep down I feel guilty. I was the one who rejected her when she wanted contact. I was the one who even prayed that she suffer, Hashem help me!

Now, in my prayers, I continually ask Hashem if I should have condoned my daughter's actions. Should I have offered her my support once her marriage was a *fait accompli?* But I had my other children to consider! I had to make it abundantly clear to them that a child who rebels against his parents like that should not expect any support! But why, oh why, didn't I pray that she do *teshuvah* and come back to our way of life? Instead, I prayed that Hashem punish her.

Rabbi Walder, there are many lessons to be learned from my story. If this could happen to us, it could happen to anyone. Mothers, if you feel that something is not right with your daughters, talk to them, ask them, help them! Don't deny it.

Rebellious teenagers who think that they can lead their lives as they wish without the advice and support of their family, please heed my story and understand that no one can face life's tribulations alone. The initial excitement of being on one's own quickly fades, to be replaced by life's harsh realities. Don't try to determine your destiny alone.

And to those parents whose children have taken such steps, I say: Use all your energy to draw your children back and not to reject them. Pray to Hashem, beg Him to act with mercy and compassion. Stand up and fight, but just be sure you are not fighting against your own interests.

Rivka has begun to talk to me now, and although we talk about her children, the seven terrible years of her marriage are still a taboo subject. I can't begin to imagine how much she suffered. However hard it was for me, at least I had a supportive family. I denied her that, and her sole companions were pain and sorrow.

On my most recent visit, as I stood up to leave, I said, "I have a birthday present for you."

"But Imma, my birthday was a few months ago," she replied, smiling faintly.

I didn't know what to reply, so I unwrapped the gift and put the jeweled heart necklace around her neck. "This was your eighteenth-birthday present," I whispered in a trembling voice.

We both broke down. We held each other close and our tears fell together as we wept bitterly for all that we had brought upon ourselves and each other these last seven years.

Those tears were a vital step toward Rivka's recovery — and mine.

I pray to Hashem that He send her a complete recovery, that she regain her wisdom, her beauty, and her love of life. I pray that my beloved firstborn daughter will return to her children and, at long last, to us.

And I pray that Hashem forgive me.

Shimke

Dear Rabbi Walder,

Although I have been a regular listener to your radio program for a long time, I only recently thought of writing to you myself.

When I heard the sad story you read recently about the Holocaust survivor, I realized I had to tell you my story — or rather, my father's.

As a young girl growing up in Israel, I knew that the Holocaust had happened, of course, but I was blissfully unaware that it had any connection to my family. My parents kept silent on the subject until they had married off their last child, and then something happened — they started to talk. And we learned of their terrible stories.

It turns out that my father lost his first wife and eight children, and my mother lost her first husband and their three children. They were both the sole survivors of their entire families. They described to us in detail the fear, the cruelty, the indescribable suffering as, one by one, their large families were wiped out. I recoiled at hearing their stories, yet I felt compelled to listen to them.

When I asked my father why they had waited all these years to tell us, he dismissed the question as if it did not need a reply, as if it were one of those questions that cannot be answered. My brothers and sister offered the commonly voiced explanation that our parents had suffered so much that by keeping their past to themselves they were protecting themselves from pain. However, I always had the feeling that they were hiding something.

Then one day my father unlocked one of the closed chambers of his heart. "I have an answer to your question," he told me. "Guilt. I think that every survivor feels guilty that he is alive. One person's death causes you sorrow. But when all your family and all your acquaintances die, you wonder why you were left alive. You are almost sorry that you did not join them. You also feel partly guilty for their deaths."

"Tell me more," I said gently.

"You can't imagine what happens to a person whose life is in constant danger," he continued. "He becomes less sensitive to others and develops animal-like instincts to stay alive. People only hear about the heroism of the survivors, but believe me — every survivor can also tell you stories of weakness, either his or other people's. I loathe the Germans for murdering our people, but I also despise them for what they inflicted on the living. They turned them into animals, human beings without dignity. Distinguished doctors and professors became petty creatures capable of trampling a child to grab a bread crumb. Pious, pure women were turned into sub-human creatures, robbed of their modesty, their feminine virtues, their internal as well as their external beauty."

My ususally reticent father now seemed unable to stop. His words poured forth. "It is hard enough to for a survivor to bear what the Germans inflicted on his beloved family. But, when he thinks back to certain situations in which circumstances forced him to act as he did, sometimes even for a few fleeting minutes, that becomes too much to bear. Although there were many instances of selflessness, there were also other instances too —" he paused. "Instances in which you had to make decisions which might save your life, but until your dying day you feel worthless, evil, and morally tainted."

I listened breathlessly as my father shared his innermost thoughts.

"Try to picture the line outside our bakery right after Pesach," my father went on. "In their rush to taste freshly baked bread, even normal people will push and shove. In the camps, we didn't fight for the finer things in life. We fought just to stay alive.

"But in the midst of this Hell," my father said, "there were exceptions. Individuals who managed to retain the spark of human decency during all their tribulations. Such a person was Reb Shimke Deutsch."

Shimke! We had been hearing about Shimke for years, long before my father told us about his experiences in the Holocaust. For instance, he always encouraged us to help others, to give to other people, "like Shimke." He tried to train us to be frugal "just like Shimke," to have nobility of spirit "just like Shimke," and to be considerate of others "just like Shimke." Who was Shimke? We didn't know. All we knew was that he was once our father's friend — in some other place, at some other time.

Now, when my father began to talk, we learned that Shimke had been incarcerated with him in the Maidanek concentration camp. Upon arrival in Maidanek, during the "Selectzia," Shimke had insisted on keeping his family together. The Nazis had other plans and signaled him and his son to go to the right, to life, whereas his wife and daughters were pointed to the left, to death. Reb Shimke went wild and the Nazis threatened to shoot him on the spot.

"Go ahead, shoot me!" he cried. Since he was at the front of the line and the Germans were not eager for panic to break out in the crowd, they gave him a kick and allowed the family to remain united.

Shimke would never push ahead of others in the line for food, which meant that he often went hungry. When he did receive his portion, he would invariably share it with others. In short, Reb Shimke was a living saint who retained his "mentschlichkeit" throughout the Holocaust.

Over the years, we had come to know Shimke well. Now we knew who he was.

"Bring up your children to be like Shimke," my father told us, "and to give of themselves to others. He was perfect. And...and I am jealous of Shimke for the way he lived." He lowered his voice. "And for how he died."

Now we learned the story of his death. Reb Shimke stole food for one of the sick inmates. This had been going on for a few days. At great personal danger, he would steal a few potatoes from the kitchen and was thus able to revive the body and soul of the dying prisoner. As the man began the slow road to recovery, the Nazis discovered what had happened. They threatened to beat the sick man if he did not divulge the identity of the inmate who had stolen food to help him. He disclosed the name, and Shimke was hanged. My father said that Shimke went to his death happy and at peace. My father was a witness that Shimke had lived and died as a true *tzaddik*.

I came to realize that the most frequently mentioned person during my entire childhood was Shimke. Now I understood why, and as he told me more and more about Shimke, I felt that my father would have happily died instead of him.

"You cannot appreciate what a blessing it is to die without any guilt feelings. Always try to do the right thing. *Always*. Then you can live without guilt. And try to educate your children to follow in the footsteps of Shimke Deutsch."

Years went by. My mother ע״ה passed away. In his golden

14

years, my father moved in with us. I tried to offer him the best possible care, and sometimes when I sat with him I would ask him to tell me more stories about Reb Shimke Deutsch and his good deeds. He complied and I got to know even more about Shimke, and also about my father's first family, the brother and sisters I would never know. I always encouraged him, and told him he shouldn't feel such guilt. After all, I said, he was powerless to prevent the death of his wife and dear children. Had he rebelled, he would have "achieved" his own death — the chopping down of the tree trunk itself and not just the precious branches. He had built his life anew, I told him, married and raised a fine Jewish family in Eretz Yisrael. Why, oh why did he have such guilt feelings?

One day, when he was eighty-seven, my father called me. He told me he felt his end was near. He kissed me, and thanked me for showing him such respect and honor.

"Now I want to tell you something I have kept secret all my life," he told me, his weak voice suddenly becoming stronger. "Surely you remember how Shimke stole some potatoes for the dying prisoner, saving his life, and then the Nazis forced that inmate to tell them who the thief was?"

"Yes," I nodded. "I remember."

"I was that inmate," he whispered. "Pray to Hashem that He forgive me."

And my father returned his soul to his Creator.

Best Friend

Dear Rabbi Walder,
I am sending you this letter after much deliberation. It is very difficult for me to be publicizing such a personal story. But I finally decided that others can learn from my story, so I put my reservations aside.

I grew up in a very special apartment building. All nine families who lived there had been childhood friends, who had gotten married around the same time. After several years they decided to purchase a plot of land together and build, with an apartment for each family. You can imagine how nice it was — the neighbors were all great friends, like family really. All the children had lots of friends their own age in the building, and we were always organizing outings and bonfires together. If my mother needed a cup of sugar, we could always run to the neighbors and borrow one. My parents were very proud of their special building, and always told people about it.

We were especially close to the family who lived above us. They were a lot like us and their children were the same ages as we were. Their daughter Sarah was my best friend as far back as I can remember. We were in the same class at school, and we were inseparable. One year we were assigned to different classes, and our parents went the principal to ask that we be placed together again. We were, and continued that way. We went to the same high school too.

Sarah was very outgoing and popular. She was a natural leader and I, a quieter and shyer type, gradually became dependent on her. She was my counselor and my confidante. We were inseparable, and I felt lost without her.

Although she was the stronger partner in our friendship, I nevertheless sensed that she needed me as much as I needed her. By nature, Sarah was a very proud girl, and would not confide in anyone for fear of being made fun of. But with me, she was not afraid to reveal her innermost feelings, because she knew she had my absolute loyalty. I took this as a great compliment and in return I shared all my thoughts with her too.

After high school, when we reached the age for *shidduchim*, we naturally told each other about each boy we went out with.

I knew a lot of girls who found their *bashert* easily, but things did not go so smoothly for me. Every time, the boy would decide "no." Three boys even gave a negative reply based only on inquiries they made about me! Twice, I got a "no" after only one date, even though the meeting had gone well and they had both seemed interested in continuing. Of course I was very upset, and I discussed the situation for hours with Sarah.

She was very understanding. She would calm me down and tell me that those boys were evidently not worthy of a wonderful girl like me.

The period of the next few months was the most depressing time I had ever experienced. I went out on countless *shidduchim* and they all ended with a negative answer. Not one "yes"! It was devastating. There's a limit to how many times a girl can hear this. My parents were at a loss too. I was a pretty and popular girl from a good family, and suddenly when it came to *shidduchim* — nobody wanted me.

Sarah was my lifesaver. She was always suggesting *shidduchim* for me, but nothing came of any of them. At that point, I saw that she was so involved in my *shidduchim* that she was neglecting her own. I should add, by the way, that her problem was the exact opposite — she had no shortage of offers but *she* always said no. Sarah was very picky.

By the time I was 23, the pattern had become predictable. I was particularly upset when I would go out three or four times with a boy, and it appeared to be going well, and then suddenly, without any explanation, the boy would call it off.

By this point several *shadchanim* had mentioned to my father that something strange seemed to be going on. It was as if something would suddenly make the boy end any *shidduch*. We couldn't imagine what this could be — there were no "family secrets" or "skeletons in the closet" which would cause this. One *shadchan* suggested that my father go and discuss the matter with a certain Rav, but he had already been to lots of *Rabbanim*!

One day I went out with a really special young man. From the start, I felt that David was right for me, and I sensed that the feeling was mutual. We met a few times, I became hopeful, and then — as usual — he dropped me. This time I was completely shattered. I spent several sleepless nights, with Sarah at my side, crying over my lot in life.

I decided to suggest him for Sarah. If I couldn't continue with him, surely she deserved someone like him. At first she wouldn't hear of it. If he didn't have the sense to choose me, she said, then she wasn't interested in meeting him. But I finally convinced her to let me suggest it. I dialed his number and told his mother that I have an excellent *shidduch* for her son. I spent the next half hour singing Sarah's praises and his mother became very interested. She made her own inquiries, and agreed.

David and Sarah went out on several dates. He was not at all certain about her, and I invested all my energy in encouraging him! We became very close! I spoke to him for hours on the phone, telling him how everyone admires Sarah, and what a wonderful girl she was. He told me about his concerns and I allayed his fears. They continued to go out, but nothing came of it.

He finally said he needed time to consider, and broke off the *shidduch* for the time being.

The following week, David's Rosh Yeshivah called my father and told him he wanted to discuss a certain matter. My father went to meet with him. The subject was David. And me.

"As you know," the Rosh Yeshivah began, "this young man went out with your daughter and then broke off the *shidduch*. He now wants to meet her again, but his parents are adamantly against it. I have discussed the matter at length with him and he is *equally* adamant to go ahead! The problem seems to be that his parents don't want him to marry a girl with a...a problematic background. I am certainly sympathetic to their concern, but since I have never met a young man as determined as David, I would like you to show me the, um, relevant documentation so that I can decide for myself how serious your daughter's condition is. Maybe then I can convince David's parents that hers was only a short-term problem."

My father was stunned. "I'm sorry, but I don't understand what you mean," he exclaimed. "What documentation? What condition can you possibly be talking about? I'm afraid I simply don't know what it is you want from me."

The Rav looked very embarrassed. "I realize this is not an easy matter for you to discuss," he said, "but the other side heard about your daughter's nervous breakdown and her subsequent hospitalization."

My father was speechless. Then he managed to utter a few words: "Are you sure we're talking about *my daughter?*"

It soon transpired that the Rosh Yeshivah was convinced that I had suffered a nervous breakdown. My father rose and walked over to the *mezuzah* on the door and kissed it. "I give you my word...with all my heart," he said, "I assure you that my daughter has never, God forbid, had any mental problems, and she has never spent one day in a hospital — any hospital! This is an outright lie, a libel! You can ask anyone who knows us — in our building, where people have known each other for forty years, or wherever you like. I am prepared to waive her right of medical confidentiality to clear her name."

The Rosh Yeshivah replied that David's parents claim to have a highly reliable source. "So let us go to them right now," my father said, "or whenever they want, in order to prove that this is totally false."

That evening, my father went to David's house with the Rosh Yeshivah. I remained at home with my mother, crying. I found it incomprehensible that anyone would spread such a rumor about me.

My father returned as white as a sheet. He looked as if he had been dealt a physical blow. He called us all together and said, "I bring you both good and bad news. The good news is that I managed to convince David's parents that you have never had any mental problem whatsoever. The bad news is that I discovered who was trying to ruin this *shidduch*." He paused for a moment. "Your best friend — Sarah!"

It took my mother and me several minutes to recover from the shock. Meanwhile my father recounted how David's parents had spoken to Sarah initially to make inquiries about me when they saw that things looked promising. She'd had only good things to say, but she'd added, in strict confidence of course, that I had suffered a severe nervous breakdown when I was 18 and had even been hospitalized. They ended the *shidduch* but David was very unhappy about it. Later, when we'd talked at length on the phone about Sarah, he'd become convinced that he had been wrong to break off the *shidduch* with me. He told his parents that he saw things in me which he hadn't seen in any of the other girls he had met, and he wanted to marry me despite my supposed mental condition! His parents thought he was being irrational. He even told his Rosh Yeshivah that if his parents forbade him to marry me, *he* would have a breakdown and then we would make a fine pair!

The Rosh Yeshivah decided to investigate the matter, and then the whole affair had come to light.

My mother began thinking about all my *shidduch* experiences, and did a little investigating on her own. We were shocked to discover that Sarah had been busy for years — whenever a *shidduch* was suggested to me, we had sent the prospective parents to Sarah for personal references! It turned out that apparently she had told everyone about my "condition." Sarah was the wall blocking my path to marriage and happiness. Did she want to keep me single as long as she was single? Was she secretly envious of me? I'll never understand it, really.

Because we wanted to be absolutely certain, we asked one of my cousins to pose as a *shadchan* and call Sarah for information about me. She had only good things to say about me, but then added, as an aside, that except for my nervous breakdown, everything was perfect. My cousin probed further and Sarah provided a "detailed report" of my illness, including the name of the hospital where I was treated! Unknown to Sarah, the conversation was taped.

The hospital provided us with a statement that I had never been treated at their institution. We gathered photographs and video films to prove that at the time Sarah said I was hospitalized, I was actually a senior counselor at a sleep-away camp! This may sound extreme, but we felt it was necessary so that David's parents would bless the *shidduch* without the slightest doubt about me. David couldn't have cared less — he told me that he'd wanted to marry me even *with* my "breakdown," but he was glad to find out that it was a lie.

We celebrated our engagement the following week. I didn't tell Sarah. She heard from someone else, and came to over to wish us *Mazal tov*. My mother greeted her and handed her a tape of her conversation with our cousin. "First listen to this," my mother told her, "and then maybe we'll talk."

Sarah never returned.

David and I have been married for three years, and have found true happiness together. It was worth waiting all those years for such a wonderful husband.

As you can imagine, my faith in other people took a tremendous blow — my best friend had betrayed me. But Hashem works in wonderful ways. Although I lost faith in people because of Sarah's betrayal, thanks to my husband's love and devotion, I learned to trust again. Nevertheless, I still shudder when I think about it.

Rabbi Walder, I want to tell your listeners the following: Be aware! Look around you. If something seems to go wrong again and again, stop and think. Maybe someone is deliberately meddling, stooping to the lowest levels to prevent your happiness. Sometimes one evil neighbor can ruin a person's entire life. I have learned that my story is not unique. I also want to tell your listeners to check and double-check every piece of information they hear, even if it appears to be true. This is especially the case if the source stresses that the information is confidential. (Sometimes the true secret in such a case is that the person is telling a lie.)

The most important lesson to be learned from my story is to deepen our *bitachon*, our trust in Hashem. All that my ex-friend did against me turned out to be for my own good — her actions actually prevented me from marrying the wrong partner, for when I finally met the right one, David, he overcame all the obstacles in our way.

My faith in Hashem has therefore become much stronger — I *thought* I was suffering, but I know now that Hashem was leading me on the path to happiness.

I imagine you are curious about what became of Sarah. I know she got engaged a year later and on the day of her wedding she sent me a note asking my forgiveness. I forgave her, but I do not think I will ever be able to understand her behavior.

For our first anniversary, I bought us a gift: a picture of a red-roofed house surrounded by a garden of flowers. A verse from *Tehillim* is written on the picture: "If Hashem will not build the house, its builders labor on it in vain."

I would add: "If Hashem wants to build the house, its destroyers labor in vain!"

The Used-Car Salesman

Dear Rabbi Walder,

My story begins thirteen years ago, when I was a used-car salesman. I was in partnership with two friends, Avi and Benny.

Before I go into the details of my story, I want to tell you a little about the world of used-car dealers. You've probably heard only bad things about these people — that they're crooks who are quite capable of selling a car minus its engine! But I can tell you as an insider that I know these people, and they just want to make a living and get a fair price — most of the time. I do admit, though, that this business is based on what we used to call "white lies." For example, a dealer will describe a car that was involved in a head-on collision as having a "slight dent." If the bodywork was bent and scraped, he might say someone gave the car a "kiss." The chassis was always in "perfect working order" and the engine looked as new as if it had just come off the assembly line.

The truth is, though, that when an individual sells his own car he also plays the same game — just on a smaller scale. He makes sure to have the engine cleaned so it really does look brand new, he washes the seats till they shine, he paints over the scratches, wipes away the oil stains and proudly declares that his car is very economical in gas usage.

Dealers just do things in a more sophisticated and "professional" way. A dealer makes most of his profits from despairing car owners who cannot sell their run-down pieces of junk. So they sell it to a dealer for 60% of its value, and he tries to get a price somewhere between 80 and 100% of its value.

There's a saying that goes: "You can't be both a saint and a used-car dealer — it's one or the other." The story I am going to tell you is the exception, perhaps.

As I mentioned, thirteen years ago I ran a used-car lot with my two partners. Business was not particularly good and we considered ourselves fortunate if we made one sale a day. We passed the time by playing cards or getting into arguments with each other. If we were really bored we would mix these two "pleasures" together.

On the day my story took place, we had an old car standing in the lot. It must have been about twenty years old. Someone had actually paid us to take it away! My partner Avi was really good with his hands and from time to time he would tinker with the car. Eventually he changed the engine block, straightened up the bodywork and painted the car. Of course he didn't forget the seat covers — you'd be amazed how many people buy a car based only on its looks or how nicely the seats are covered. Avi converted that old wreck into a stunning-looking car!

One day we were sitting around, bored as usual, when a very religious Jew walks in and says he's looking to buy a cheap car. I took one look at him and knew that we were onto a good deal. He looked really naive, the type of person who probably had no idea how to raise the hood of a car — and he had come into our lot to swell our bank balance. I felt that our prayers had been answered!

We immediately showed him the renovated car and offered

it to him for a hefty price. Our profit would be fantastic. We showed him only what we wanted him to see, and he was really impressed by the "clean" engine. He was more enthusiastic about the car than *we* dared be; in fact he was so enthusiastic that we even regretted the "low" offer we had made him. He said he would return with the money the next day, and we were left hoping that he wouldn't change his mind.

True to his word, he arrived by cab the next morning. As he got out, he took a large stroller out of the trunk which looked suitable for a baby. To our surprise, he carried an older boy, about nine years old, out of the car and sat him in the stroller. He was a handsome young boy but his eyes were sad. I saw that his legs were paralyzed and there was also something strange-looking about the way his arms rested at his side.

My partners welcomed the father as if they were old friends and gave him VIP treatment. Somehow I got stuck with the boy.

"What's your name?" I tried to start up a conversation.

"Michael Feinberg."

"What school do you go to?" I immediately regretted my question. Maybe he was too handicapped to attend school,

"I go to *cheder* — I'm in the fourth grade." Michael told me he loved school, that the other children helped him whenever possible, and he had lots of friends. We continued talking for a while and then the conversation turned to the car. He looked at it with his large eyes and asked me all about it. What's its mileage, he wanted to know. Is the engine in good condition and can they be sure that it will never break down?

I gave him the usual answers but deep down I began to feel guilty. It's one thing to smoothtalk a regular customer but it's just not right with such a sweet child, especially a handicapped one. From the office I could hear them laughing and I guessed that my partners were exerting their charms on Mr. Feinberg, trying to get him to buy all sorts of extras. I felt bad for him.

And I had every reason to feel bad for him. I knew the car he was about to buy. I knew that within two days it would make its first visit to a mechanic because of the gas cable which Avi had patched together. The next thing to go would be the gear stick, then the clutch which had already done a lifetime's work and was now useless. I could almost guarantee that a week later the whole engine would go up in smoke, and it wouldn't be worth repairing.

I couldn't bear to think that Michael would not get to school because his father would be too busy running off to the mechanic, and he maybe wouldn't get any toys or books from his parents because all their money would be thrown away on repairs.

I took a deep breath. "Michael," I said, "I am going to be perfectly frank with you. Don't buy this car — it's no good and will only cause you trouble. Don't tell my friends what I've just told you — just call your father over here and try and talk him out of this 'bargain' before it's too late."

Michael's eyes opened wide. "Why are you telling me all this?"

That's some smart kid, I thought to myself. "Because I wouldn't want to cheat a sweet kid like you. I might be short of cash but I still have a heart. I'm going into the office now. I'll call your father over here, and *you* tell him you don't want the car."

With a nod of his head, Michael let me know he understood. I ran over to the office and told Mr. Feinberg that his son was calling him. He immediately hurried over to Michael, who spoke quietly to him. I saw that the father dismissed Michael's concerns with an impatient wave of his arm, and he turned back towards the office. Michael called him back again, and the scene repeated itself. This happened several more times, and then Mr. Feinberg wheeled his son into the office.

In a joking tone of voice he faced the three of us. "My son has suddenly decided that he doesn't want this car. It's certainly news to me that a child decides instead of his father what car to buy and at what price!"

My friends said they couldn't agree more — it was up to the father to decide. Mr. Feinberg didn't notice the furious looks Benny and Avi were giving me. They immediately put two and two together and realized that I had opened my mouth to Michael.

Avi sat Mr. Feinberg down and told him to start counting out the cash. He started counting.

I was in a real dilemma. The deal was about to take place and I just couldn't allow that to happen.

"Mr. Feinberg!" I cried. "I really think you should take Michael's wishes into consideration. After all, he is handicapped."

The three of them stared at me and Avi asked if I had lost my mind. "This customer is about to conclude the deal of a lifetime."

Benny shot me a look that could kill.

I plucked up every ounce of courage that I had, and said: "I am a partner in this business, and I do not authorize this sale. This car is unsuitable for Mr. Feinberg!"

Before they had a chance to reply I reeled off a list of the car's problems: the gears, the clutch, the engine, and even the gas cable. I didn't bother looking at Avi and Benny — I could guess what the look on their faces was. Once I finished my speech, Mr. Feinberg said politely that he wanted to think the matter over, and left the office with his son. He went to hail a taxi, and I was left alone with Benny and Avi.

It doesn't take much imagination to figure out what happened next. Let's just say that all the dealers from neighboring lots were called in to try and calm things down. When that didn't work and the brawl became life-threatening, the police were called. That is most unusual in our trade, because once the police arrive, they start asking all kinds of questions. It goes without saying that dealers are not particularly willing to provide the police with certain answers. But in this case they were certainly needed — as were the two ambulances which took both Benny and me off to the hospital.

In the trade, everyone condemned me, and from their point of view they were right. With a few words, I had ruined a good business deal and deprived my partners of much-needed cash. Much worse was the fact that I had ruined their good name and given them the reputation of being swindlers, and that was unforgivable.

We arranged to go to arbitration. The mediators sympathized with my motives but they said that it was unacceptable to ruin business transactions by letting personal feelings interfere. Although I had been honest with a customer, at the same time I had caused my partners to lose money and I had spoiled their good reputation. It was decided that I pay them compensation. I paid up and thus ended our partnership.

Life became one long hardship. I couldn't find a job, and it was very difficult to provide for my wife and children. Friends who heard of the hard time I was going through criticized me for what I had done, but I would not listen to them. I felt that I had done the right thing and that Hashem would reward me one day.

My wife was a pillar of support and always encouraged me. Women possess a built-in sense of right and wrong which is sometimes lacking in men. If I had broken up with Avi and Benny because of a petty fight, she might have been angry with me, but she knew what had happened and stood behind me.

For ten years I did not hold down a steady job, but I always worked hard when I could, and sometimes I would deal in second-hand cars on the side. Somehow we managed to make ends meet.

Two years ago, I was having a particularly difficult time, and a friend told me about a job that was being advertised. A well-known association that helps needy people was looking for someone to be in charge of their fleet of cars. My friend warned me not to get my hopes up, though, because there were several other very experienced candidates for the job, including a car mechanic. I figured I had nothing to lose — if Hashem wants me to have this job, then the job will be mine — so I sent in an application form and I was called for an interview.

I sat and faced eight men who were sitting around a table, and they all fired questions at me. They were especially interested in my experience. I listed my previous jobs, and in the middle I just stopped. I could see that I was not making a good impression — how could I, when I had worked at so many different places? I felt that they were continuing the interview just to be polite. I had been in this situation so many times, it was *déjà-vu*. Finally they called an end to the interview and asked me to wait outside for an answer.

For 25 minutes I waited. I couldn't imagine what was taking so long. I was about to leave, since I felt I just couldn't face being turned down this time, when I was called back into the room. A silver-haired man, the association chairman, asked me if I had told them about *all* my previous jobs. I realized what he was getting at — I hadn't told them about my work in the used-car lot. I felt they were out to embarrass me for some reason, and I felt like replying that I was not under cross-examination — but he had a friendly voice and manner and so I answered him politely.

"We are looking for someone who is extremely trustworthy," the man told me. "The successful candidate will be in charge of an annual budget of thousands of dollars and we are looking for a reliable person."

I felt my blood was boiling. "And just because I was a used-car dealer, you can't trust me with the job? Have you tried to find out what kind of person I am? How can you make such generalizations?"

The man smiled. "We did indeed make our inquiries," he said quietly. "And among the things we learned is that about ten years ago you refused to sell a car to a potential customer.

"That man, Mr. Feinberg, is sitting right next to you."

I turned and realized I was looking at Mr. Feinberg, Michael's father! I would never have recognized him as the young "greenhorn" I had dealt with. He was now a stout man with a long, graying beard. But he had recognized me.

I was speechless.

"Mr. Feinberg told us the story, and we are convinced that you are the right man for the job..."

He spelled out the details of my salary and terms of the job — but I wasn't listening. I was thinking about what had just hit me: how Hashem was telling me that He knew how I had suffered all these years and that I'd nevertheless never once regretted my good deed. Now He was compensating me, and in good measure.

I really feel that Hashem is with me. It's not just the good salary, but I now have a respectable position and my new colleagues are really special people. They arranged for me to meet Michael Feinberg again. He can walk, but with difficulty, but he's really improved since I last saw him. He is a tall *yeshivah bachur* now and he is so respectful to me. Most people around here know about the connection between us.

My new job has brought other changes in our life too. I have become more religious — no one forced me, it all came from within. I was simply attracted to my colleagues' way of life; they are all really special people. I find it difficult to be completely observant, but we do keep Shabbos at home. My wife has always lit Shabbos candles, but that was all we kept. Now my children have begun to attend a religious school, and all of us are learning more and more.

Rabbi Walder, we listen to your program every week and think it is great. I hope you will read out my story and that your listeners will be encouraged to be honest and straight and never regret doing the right thing. If I remember correctly, it's written in our Scriptures, "Cast your bread upon the waters and in the end you will find it."

A Ray of Light

D
ear Rabbi Walder,
I am going through a particularly hard time right now. My life has never been a bed of roses, though. As long as I can remember, I have been a nobody. No one ever cared about me. I am slightly disabled and that hasn't helped matters much. I've never done any harm to anyone, but there is nothing particularly great about me either. I remember once when I was a child, a classmate looked me straight in the eye and said, "Shuki, you are so ordinary and boring. Who would want you in our crowd?"

No one else was ever so blunt, but I got the hint — no one would ever be interested in me.

School was tough. I can't recall a single Rav or teacher who was kind to me. Quite the contrary — I felt constantly insulted by them in every way. I thought they probably couldn't stand to look at me. Sometimes I would get so jealous when a teacher would smile kindly at the boy sitting next to me, and then he would turn to me and in a split second his whole facial expression would change to impatience and irritation. I don't even know if the teachers were aware of what they did, but I certainly was and it broke my heart.

At home things were not much better, but that subject is so painful that I would rather not go into it at all.

When I was 24, I got married. I was very hopeful that I had finally found someone who would love me. The problem was that I didn't know that in order to receive you have to give. I assumed that my wife would love me and appreciate me just because she was my wife. By the time I understood that I also had to work at the relationship, it was too late, and we got divorced after five years of marriage. I have no bad feelings towards her. She probably suffered as much as I did. She spent five years of her life with a husband who did nothing to improve himself or to make her happy. The only good thing that resulted from our marriage was the two wonderful daughters who were born to us.

By the time I reached the age of thirty, I was resigned to living the rest of my life alone and friendless. I even coined a phrase to myself that described my life: "life in the shadow of others." I was afraid to stand out in a group of people because I felt so inferior and worthless; I preferred to hide in their shadow. My daughters were the only light in my life.

Last year I got a job at a large supermarket. It involved routine work — stocking shelves, doing deliveries, etc. This job suited me because I was not conspicuous and customers took no notice of me. They wouldn't even stop and ask me where to find a particular product — it was as if I had blended into the background. I was invisible. I was not a person.

One day a new manager, Chanan, took over at the supermarket. He was a few years younger than I, and he seemed like a nice guy. From the start I made every effort not to be noticed, but he found me. He was extremely friendly.

At first I figured that he just wanted to start off on the right foot with his workers, but he turned out to be a real angel. It is difficult to describe how kind he was to each worker. Every morning he would greet us with a smile and the words, "Good morning, how are you today?" He would give me a friendly pat on the back and treat me as if we were equals. In fact, he was very respectful towards me. If I protested, he'd say that I deserved it because I was his "elder"! Chanan promoted me and gave me more respectable duties. He saw me as a loyal worker.

It didn't take long before all the workers in the supermarket admired our new boss. We were simple people — food workers, check-out clerks, cleaners — but we all realized that Chanan was a God-fearing man with a heart of gold. He really cared about us. He treated everyone equally and didn't discriminate against anyone because of their looks or their brains or anything. I must admit I had a feeling that he was extra kind to me because he suspected that life had dealt me a few blows. Out of gratitude, I would have done anything he asked, but he was so considerate, he never even asked me to work overtime. When he saw that a particular task was difficult, he would come over himself to help me or call another worker.

It is difficult for me to put down on paper my feelings for Chanan. Simply put, he was the best person I'd ever met. The best person in the whole world! He was the first, and only, person in my life who had ever treated me as an equal and who respected each and every person he met.

Then disaster struck. Rabbi Walder, do you know how it feels when you can't write about a terrible event? It is almost impossible for me to describe the events of that tragic day. Chanan was driving a fork-lift truck. I had always warned him to be careful because it looks like an innocent toy but it is in fact a dangerous machine. As he was driving, the blades got stuck in a concrete block and the truck overturned, crushing Chanan underneath.

Chanan died, leaving behind a wife and an unborn child. I feel like life is over for me also — the only person who ever treated me with respect is gone. His funeral was attended by thousands of people. They were all crying as if they had lost their own brother. All the speakers talked about his special character. Afterwards we workers stayed behind and cried at the freshly dug grave.

I do not understand why Hashem took away the only ray of light in my dark world. I cry for Chanan all the time and miss him terribly.

Rabbi Walder, the world would be a better place if more people were like Chanan. He befriended everyone. Do you know what a *tzaddik* he was? If he wanted to call our attention to something about Jewish law, he would do it in a quiet, gentle way, without embarrassing us or showing us how smart he was! I am sure Hashem has a place of honor in Gan Eden for Chanan.

I feel it is important to tell people about Chanan's qualities so that maybe, just maybe, those of us still in this world will be able to learn from his deeds.

Heart of Gold

D ear Rabbi Walder,
I've been wanting to write to you for some time and tell you my story, but I couldn't see myself writing to a radio program. The letter you read on your last program, about the man who brought happiness to everyone around him and then he died, really touched me. I know how the fellow who wrote the letter felt — finally someone was kind to him and it changed his life. So I said to myself, that's it, I just have to write to Rabbi Walder with my story.

I am now forty-four years old, but I've been through so much in my life I think I could easily be seventy. From the age of ten I was out on the street and I never really went to school. I spent a good number of years behind bars. I'm not going to disclose my real name — it wouldn't mean anything to you, but in the underworld I'm well-known. It would be easy for me to come up with lots of excuses to explain why I didn't grow up to be an honest person — I could tell you about the lack of opportunities in my life, and this and that, but when all is said and done, if you break the law, you're a criminal. And that's exactly what I was.

Over the years I was involved in petty crime — mainly thefts and break-ins — but I also got caught for committing armed robbery once and then I landed a heavy jail sentence. However, I never hurt a single person and I steered clear of drugs.

Shortly after I completed my last jail sentence, about six years ago, I began planning the robbery of a jewelry store in Jerusalem. I had received information that a large sum of money and lots of jewelry were kept in the store. Since it was situated on a quiet side street, I knew I could walk in, hold up the owner, and easily carry off the goods without drawing too much attention to myself. As part of my planning, I decided to pay a visit to the shop to check it out — the layout, the salesperson, and the location of the safe. You have to be well-prepared for this kind of thing.

Early one evening, shortly before closing time, I went to get a good look at the place. The owner, an older man, was alone in the shop and was friendly and polite. I asked to see a necklace "for my wife" (what a lie!). He showed me all kinds of necklaces and even opened the safe to bring out different styles. What a reckless thing to do! I could have easily ransacked the safe, but no — everything has its time and place and I was there to plan, not to act.

This gentleman asked about my wife — how was he to know that she only existed in my imagination! So I began to spin a story, as I was pretty good at doing. This time I came up with the tale that we were a young couple without a penny to our name, but that I'd managed to scrape together a few dollars to buy her a surprise birthday gift. This seemed to really touch the man, and he asked me what work I do. I replied that I was unemployed. (Really, I had never held a job in my life, unless of course you consider my "profession" to be work.) Now this fellow started to take pity on me and tried to offer me encouragement, so I decided it was time to get out of there before I actually began to like him.

He turned to me, looked me straight in the eye and said, "Listen, young man — you seem like a talented fellow who just needs a little help. I am willing to lend you some money so you can invest in a little business, possibly jewelry, which would provide you with a living."

My mouth dropped open and before I could utter a sound he hurried to the safe, took out some money, and slapped a thick wad of bills down on the counter. "Here's ten thousand dollars for you," he announced, smiling.

"Are you crazy?" I asked him. "How can you lend money to a complete stranger? What do you know about me?"

"I've been in business for forty-eight years," he replied, "and I've got a good eye for judging people. I can see that you're a decent person with a good heart. I trust you to return the money when you can."

I was flabbergasted. In my entire life no one had ever trusted me. Not even with one dollar.

"Now, listen, friend, you're getting carried away," I told him. "We've never met before, and you are about to give me all that money? How do you know that you will ever get it back?"

"Young man, stop asking questions," he said. "I can see straight through you. Straight to your heart. And I see you have a heart of gold — 24 karats, just like my necklaces. You are an honest man — I do not have the slightest doubt that you will return the money."

I started thinking, Wow this guy is for real! I don't even have to risk a robbery. I'll just stand here, get the cash, and run for it. What could be better than that?

Yet — it wasn't so simple. If this man was willing to trust me, then he was now somewhat of a friend. Could I really steal from a friend who trusted me? I decided that I would be better off to refuse the money and come back next week and simply steal it. But the speed with which he handed me those dollar bills confused me, and I let him do it.

As I left his store and hurried away, my heart was pounding. When I got home, I broke down and wept like a small child. Had anyone ever believed in me before today? What a joke! Had any person ever trusted me? True, in the underworld everyone knew that I kept my word. But what does it mean that thieves trust each other? They trust each other to divide up the stolen goods equally!

And here was this honest, kind man, the type of person who was never, ever, a part of my life, and he trusted and respected me.

I determined to pay him back, down to the very last cent.

Well, Rabbi Walder, for the fun of it I bought some goods, and sold them for a profit. I continued until I had tripled my initial investment. Four months later I returned to the shop and put ten thousand dollars on the counter, plus two thousand in interest. But he refused to take the interest! "Do I look like a person who takes interest?" he said angrily. I asked him to take it as a token of my respect, but he wouldn't agree.

Once again I asked him how he had dared give such a large amount of money to someone he didn't even know.

"As you get older," he said, smiling warmly at me, "you get to know more about life. As soon as I looked at you I knew that you were a decent man who wanted to earn an honest living. I could see that things were not easy for you, and I just decided to give you a chance. Now, young man, go and make a living to support your family. And make sure you always come here to buy jewelry for your wife!"

What an answer! What a man!

I left the shop with tears in my eyes and joy in my heart, and I knew then what I wanted to become — an honest and decent person. I thought about how to go about doing this, and I decided to enroll in a yeshivah. I began to study Torah, and over the course of time I became a ba'al teshuvah. This was no easy task and sometimes I felt myself slipping back to my old ways, but I always managed to get back on track. Eventually the rabbis in the yeshivah found a wife for me. We were complete opposites — she was innocent, modest, bashful, and undemanding. I felt as if Hashem was sending me the gift of happiness straight from Heaven.

The wedding ring was purchased from "my jeweler." (I had to tell him that I wanted to give my wife an even nicer ring than she already had. After all, he thought that I was already married and I couldn't tell him that it was the first wedding ring.)

We got married and one year later we celebrated the birth of our daughter. I bought my wife a gift of a beautiful necklace — needless to say, purchased from "my jeweler." It cost a pretty penny, and believe me I would have loved to buy an even more expensive one.

Every now and again friends from my past would visit and suggest doing a "job," but I refused to have anything to do with crime. At first they got annoyed, but eventually they accepted my new way of life and realized that it was all over. I was out of their world.

My wife didn't ask me about my past, but I think she was clever enough to understand, just by looking at the kind of friends I used to keep.

Two years later we were blessed with the birth of our first son. What joy we felt! We made a big celebration for his *bris*, attended by my Rabbis and friends, both from the past and the present. But one friend was not invited. I was too frightened to invite "my jeweler" in case someone would accidentally blurt out how long I had been married, or he might spot some suspicious-looking characters and wonder about me. Nevertheless, the next day I went to him to buy my wife a present.

As soon as I stepped into the shop, I saw that something was wrong. He was not a young man, but he had suddenly aged greatly.

"What's the matter, Papa?" (That's what I called him.)

He began to cry and was unable to speak. I put my arm around him and tried to calm him down. Finally he managed a few words.

"You don't want to know what happened," he began. "There was a break-in last week and my safe was ransacked. Everything went — a lifetime's savings, jewels I had purchased or which I had bought on credit, jewelry that people had brought in to be repaired, and thousands of dollars in cash. I am completely ruined. I'll be in debt as long as I live. Take a good look at me — an impoverished ruined man."

As I watched him crying and suffering, I was filled with hate towards the person who was capable of committing such a despicable act, who had ruined the life of this wonderful man. What a heartless deed! Then it struck me that this is exactly what I had planned to do not so many years earlier. I was also a heartless person, then — or was I just plain stupid? I bought a large piece of jewelry, and told him, "Be strong, Papa, and I promise you that everything will work out in the end."

He replied tearfully, "You're a good man. If only others were like you."

As I left the shop, I thought about what he said — if only others were like me! The heartless thief was indeed just like me — like I was then. I decided on a plan of action.

I went to pay a visit to some former "friends" who were quite surprised to see me walk in, with my beard and yarmulke. They had long since gotten used to the idea that I had left the world of crime. In an authoritative tone of voice, I informed them that within one week I wanted to know who had robbed a particular jeweler. They took one look at me and recognized the expression on my face. They knew, in the old days, that this meant that I was angry. That's what had given me my standing in the underworld — people knew that once I was angry and set my mind on sòmething, nothing stood in my way.

Two days later I got the information. The thief was a strong and dangerous man, and it would be no pleasure dealing with him. I went to his house and asked to speak with him. He knew my name and did not turn me away. I spoke to him in his "professional" language and informed him that I expected the stolen goods to be returned to their owner before Shabbos, or else he would have to reckon with me.

He told me it sounded as if I were declaring war. "War" in the underworld means one thing — very dirty business.

"Think what you want," I replied, "but those goods must be returned before the end of the week."

He suggested that we go to an "arbitrator" to settle the matter.

We went to a well-known figure in the world of crime, and it was obvious that he didn't take my side. He wanted to know why I was mixing into someone else's business. If this "job" had been on my turf, he said, it would have been my right to demand a cut. However, since I had left the "business" I had no right to interfere.

Then I took the plunge and told them the story of the jeweler. The truth. The whole story. I risked being judged a "softie" in their minds, which was not exactly a plus in that world. But I went ahead and told them all about how I had planned to rob him but he'd lent me money and put his full trust in me, and that was how he really set me on the straight path.

"It's all thanks to him," I said, "that I became an honest person, discovered a life based on Torah, and met my wife. This man saved my life and I am indebted to him." Then I added, "Besides, if it weren't for him, chances are that this area would still be 'my territory' and so anything you'd do would have to be done with my approval!"

To my surprise, both of them were impressed by my story. They asked me lots of questions, and the thief said that had he known about it he wouldn't have targeted this particular jeweler. I threw in a few gentle hints that this was a matter of life and death for me, and if it took "war" to settle it — well, that was fine with me.

The arbitrator took each of us aside separately for a few minutes and then gave his verdict to the thief: "I am assuming that he [meaning me] is still in charge of this territory and so you would have had to get his OK to carry out your job. Since you didn't — you have to give him all the money and he has to give you a ten percent cut."

He was not pleased with this judgment, which left him with only eighty grand instead of eight hundred, but he knew you don't mess around with the arbitrator. He promised to return the goods and cash before Shabbos and that's what happened — two messengers turned up at my house with suitcases containing the booty.

I still had to figure out how to make up the missing eighty thousand dollars. I withdrew all my savings — fifty thousand dollars — and took out a loan for another thirty thousand. On Saturday night as soon as Shabbos was over, I went to the jeweler's house with the two suitcases and a note. I rang the doorbell and ran away. From my hiding place I saw him open the door and take in the suitcases.

When I got home, I knew that I no longer had any assets and that I had a substantial debt, but my heart was overflowing with joy. My wife was waiting up for me. "Your husband is now a *tzaddik*," I told her. "I have just done true *teshuvah* for all my past deeds."

She did not ask me anything, but by the look on her face I knew that she believed me. May Hashem bless her — I don't know how I deserve such a special and devout wife.

I work steadily and make a good living — not as much as I did in "the old days," but I am content with my lot. I thank Hashem for what he has sent me, for my beloved wife and my wonderful children — and especially for those five minutes when someone believed in me and it changed my life.

Woman of Valor

Dear Rabbi Walder,
My friends and I all make sure never to miss your program. The letter you read last night about a criminal who became a *ba'al teshuvah* and did a particularly noble act was very moving.

I was especially touched by a minor detail in the story, something that surely not all your listeners noticed. Did you realize how he praised his wife? "A *tzadekes*"; "may Hashem bless her"; "I don't deserve such a wife." I am sure many women who heard him wished they had a husband like that.

Rabbi Walder, this is just an introduction to the story of my marriage.

I grew up in a traditional home in small moshav in the south of the country. It was a simple, warm home in which we respected Jewish tradition but were not learned enough to understand the religious practices that we kept. In high school and in teacher's seminary afterwards, I became more religious. Then I was introduced to Eli, a young man from a good family. I liked him and thought he was really special. We decided to get married right away. My parents were not so sure about the match, but they gave us their blessings.

Right after our wedding, I began to see things that I hadn't seen before. Eli had trouble keeping a job and was often unemployed. He would sleep till late morning or early afternoon, depending on how you look at it, and then would simply walk out of the house. He would hang out with his buddies, who were as irresponsible as he was, and would come home whenever he felt like it.

The years went by. Occasionally he would get interested in some failing business venture and, despite my warnings, he would invest in the business which would soon fall apart, leaving us with large debts.

Five children were born to us, and the entire burden of our livelihood, the children's education, and running the household rested squarely on my shoulders. My husband came and went as he pleased.

Eli never behaved badly to me or to our children, but as time passed, he simply didn't have much to do with our lives. I began to treat him as another child — there really was something childish in his behavior. He was easily insulted, and I decided he just had a weak character and was unable to face up to even the smallest difficulties.

When he did talk, Eli would claim that I tried to run his life for him. I guess there is some truth in that, even though I felt I had no other choice. All I was doing was running our household. Somebody had to. Whenever he was home, I would point out his shortcomings, so that he would not be too much of an influence on the children.

In fact, the children got along well with their father. When I criticized him, he would always remind me of how the children loved him, and I would retort, "Are you surprised? How many other children are 'lucky' enough to have a father who is on their level?"

Finally the day came when I decided to ask for a divorce. Eli

46

didn't agree. Why should he, I told myself bitterly — our house is his 5-star hotel. Why should he give it up? Eli urged me to try to make things better and work towards reconciliation.

And so, we went from one marriage counselor to another, but none were able to help us. In fact, most of them recommended that we get divorced. After three years of separation, my husband gave me a *get*. I assured him that I held nothing against him and that he could have unlimited visiting rights with the children. When I got my *get*, I felt free. I would like to stress again that Eli was not a bad person. He simply was not what I felt I deserved.

A year later Eli remarried. I was a little surprised, but was happy for him nevertheless. I had never really hated him, after all. However, I did feel sorry for his new wife — poor woman, I told myself, she doesn't yet know what she's let herself in for. Some time later I met his new wife, Rina. She was very friendly to me, and I saw that she was a nice person. As she spoke, I realized that she harbored no bad feelings towards me, which rather surprised me since I was sure that Eli had spoken badly about me to her. But apparently not — she said something about how people are just sometimes unsuitable for each other. Plain and simple. I agreed, and found myself telling her what a good heart Eli has. I was telling her the truth, but I didn't add that it was the only good thing I had to say about him!

Here and there, over the next few months, I heard various things about Eli, and it appeared that he was becoming a changed person. He now held a steady job and was making a decent living. He would come straight home at the end of a day's work, and gradually stopped hanging out with his cronies. My children told me that their father now studied Torah at the local *kollel* with a *chavrusa* in the evenings, and that he was taking an active interest in their studies. I was quite amazed, but at the same time somewhat uneasy. I just couldn't fathom such a change!

I ran into Rina every so often, and she always praised me for having brought up my children so well. It was a pleasure to have them over, she told me, as they were so polite and tidy. Then she praised Eli and said what a good and special man he was. She wasn't being spiteful at all, and I realized that.

Fifteen years have gone by since then. Four of my five children are married. Eli has undergone a complete metamorphosis. He is a serious, responsible, mild-mannered person who is devoted to his wife, to our children, and to their four children. He has always been punctual with his child-support payments and never caused me any trouble.

Now my children are grown, and a stage in my life has ended. I have begun to face the fact that for years I immersed myself in the details of raising my family and running my home, and never really dealt with my emotions. Maybe I didn't want to confront the truth. For all the years of my marriage I wondered how it could be that I, the perfect wife in my own eyes, who managed a perfect home, was married to a "nobody." And then I began to wonder how it could be that the minute he was set free of me, he became a *mentsch!*

Now I am allowing myself to think about many things, and deep down, I know the answer. I learned it from my conversations with Rina.

I used to search for reasons to respect and admire my husband, and I was never able to find a reason — not as a breadwinner, or a Torah scholar, or even as a responsible husband — no reason at all! Finally, and worst of all, I even thought that his good heart was due to his foolishness.

Rina, on the other hand, admired him for every little thing. Once she told me that they went to Tiberias on vacation and rented a motor boat on Lake Kinneret. "You should have seen how he steered that boat," she told me. "It was something out of this world! He was the fastest on the lake and the children were so excited and proud of him."

When I heard that, I thought bitterly, Now that's a great reason to admire your husband — he's a good sailor! I was full of contempt. I saw, though, that Rina admired everything Eli did and never criticized him.

Even when she had something negative to say about him, she couched it in such gentle and sympathetic terms that it didn't seem bad at all. I remember when they were newly married, she once told me that he slept a lot. "Poor fellow," she said, almost in tears. "He's just doesn't have strength. Every day I pray for him, that he will be strong. In the meantime, I try to make sure that he's not disturbed, if he needs the rest so badly." She had such a special way of looking at everything.

I have spent many hours comparing my attitude to Eli with Rina's. The truth stares me in the face. I was a critical, cynical wife who was forever lashing out at him, and I now realize that there was no way he could *ever* have become a *mentsch* while he was married to me. I demanded results from him without any input on my part. I gave him no credit at all; quite the contrary, I wanted him to gain stature in my eyes without allowing him the possibility to do so.

Every so often we meet at *simchas* and I can see how content he is and how much he admires Rina. She fully deserves it. When I read the verse, "A [woman's] wisdom has built her house" (*Mishlei* 9:1), I think of her.

Don't think I feel that Rina took my husband away from me. I would never have been able to change my attitude towards him, and if we had stayed together, we both would have been worse off!

I have learned from Rina that if you want to change somebody, you can't do it with snide comments, insults, and rejection. The only way to succeed is by giving — unconditionally and without expecting immediate results. I think of Rina when I read *Eishes Chayil* — especially the words, "She did him good and never evil all the days of her life."

Pay Them Back!

Dear Rabbi Walder,
     I recently listened to your program in which you read the letter from the woman who prayed that something bad should happen to her daughter who had shamed the family and hurt them. Those prayers were answered. This gave me the impetus to write down my own on-going story and mail it to you. I have never told it to anyone.

Today I am 33 years old, but my story begins twenty years ago when I finished elementary school and went to high school. I was a lively girl, and well-liked by all. I come from a good family and my parents are wonderful, decent people. Until I reached high school I never encountered any difficulties at home or socially.

All that changed when I went to high school. We were five girls who came from the same elementary school, and we constituted the largest group in the new class. Rabbi Walder, you have often talked about the move to a new setting, and how new friendships and alliances are formed and things never remain the same. At the start of the school year, the future looked bright. I made lots of new friends and felt good.

Then two of my new classmates began picking on me. I've never understood why. They somehow succeeded in turning the whole class against me. They would insult me in public, mock me, and do everything possible to upset me. Every morning I would wake up and ask myself what new form of torture they had in store for me that day. These two scheming girls were relentless in their cruelty.

I did not know how to deal with such a situation. I had never encountered intentional cruelty. I tried sending other girls to them, to ask them to leave me alone, but they sent back insulting and hurtful replies. My biggest mistake was asking my homeroom teacher to intervene on my behalf. When she tried, they looked at her innocently and just said that I must be a disturbed person if I imagined that people are out to get me. As far as I was concerned, they were two murderers, killing me with a slow, painful death. In a year they utterly destroyed the self-confidence of a lifetime.

My parents couldn't understand what was happening to me, and somehow I was ashamed to tell them the extent of my terrible situation.

Eventually the whole class was on their side. I did not know if it was because the other girls were too frightened to stand up to these two or if they just got drawn in.

On one occasion I decided to confront them myself. That incident is as fresh in my memory as if it had happened yesterday. I stood in the doorway of the games room and waited until most of the girls had left. I asked one girl to call my two tormentors over, but they replied that they couldn't be bothered to speak to me. I asked her to call them again and ask them to spare a few minutes of their time for me. I heard laughter coming from the games room: "Tell her that we don't have any spare time for crazies!"

I entered the lion's den myself then, and said that I wanted to speak to them. No reply was forthcoming. Tears sprang from my eyes and, choked by sobs, I begged them to speak to me for five minutes. They actually took pleasure in seeing me cry.

"Before you know it, she'll be groveling at our feet and kissing the earth we walk on," one of them sneered to her friend and pointed in my direction.

At that point I realized that it was pointless to try. Even if they would deign to speak to me, nothing I could say would melt their hearts of stone. I turned to leave the room and then, without intending to do so, I started speaking from the bottom of my wounded heart: "Since you are not prepared to listen to me," I cried, "Hashem will listen from Above! He sees the abuse I have suffered from you, and He knows that I am powerless to stop it. Please Hashem, *pay them back for their actions*, please stop my torment!"

They burst out laughing. They had succeeded in robbing me of the little self-respect I still possessed. I returned home broken and crushed in spirit, wanting nothing more than for my miserable life to end.

I spent the next few nights pouring my heart out to Hashem, crying that I had no strength left in me and begging Him to act on my behalf. I told Him that He is the Boss of the world and He cannot allow His creations to be so cruel to each other. I still kept this from my parents, who could see that something was bothering me, but didn't know what, or if they should interfere. In those days I felt that my belief in Hashem was my only source of strength and so I turned to Him alone. I begged Him to help me.

A month passed and out of the blue, one of my tormentors was expelled from school. This was a real scandal because she was considered an outstanding student. Rumors abounded as to the reason and it turned out that her good behavior had just been a facade. This was nothing new to me, and in fact none of the girls were really surprised.

I felt that Hashem had answered my prayers. One of my tormentors was gone. However, my troubles were not yet over — her friend did not leave me in peace. In fact, she bothered me twice as much as the two of them had previously. Whereas before she had "only" insulted me personally and talked badly about me to my classmates, she now spread the word throughout the whole school. It is bad enough to suffer within a small group but when everybody considers you to be crazy, that is too much to bear.

I sent her a note asking whether she wasn't afraid that she would receive her punishment from Hashem just like her friend had. She sent back a derisory note saying that I would rue the day her friend was expelled because she would ensure that I would now suffer threefold. Those were her exact words.

She was true to her word. Each day she would tear me to pieces and shatter my soul anew. I became a broken and frightened person, an emotional invalid. A once happy, carefree, and respected girl was now a suffering, haggard, and suspicious wreck who detested her very life.

Once again I turned to my one true friend — Hashem. My tears flowed like water as I entreated Him to rid me of my terrible suffering because I could not bear it anymore.

A mere six weeks after the first girl was expelled, a terrible tragedy occurred in the second girl's family. She lost more than one member of her immediate family in a disaster. I cannot go into details because then your listeners might recognize who I am talking about since the tragedy reached the headlines.

Rabbi Walder, as soon as I heard about the tragedy I felt that it was all due to me. To be exact, I was absolutely convinced that I had brought this about. Let me tell you that I didn't feel any relief or feeling of revenge. This was a tragedy of such magnitude that I only felt worse than I ever had. I kept on asking myself, "What have I done?" I hoped no one would make a connection between what I had said to the girls two months earlier and blame me for the tragedy. I felt that Hashem somehow blamed me for it too.

When she got up from the *shivah* she returned to school and, unbelievably, she continued to torment me. However, her actions no longer had the power to hurt me because I, and all my fellow students, now had great pity for her and were no longer afraid of her behavior. I think she must have realized that I was unaffected by her. A year later, more changes occurred in her family and as a result she left our high school and moved to a different city. I breathed one huge sigh of relief.

Rabbi Walder, I have never told this story to anyone because I am angry at myself and blame myself partly for what happened to the two girls. However, the main reason that I've never shared my story is that I am frightened of people's sarcastic reaction — they might say about me, "Since when does she have a direct line to Hashem?!" All these years I have kept silent.

I have come to the conclusion that when people are in desperate straits, in a hopeless situation, their *tefillos* have an especially strong power. This should act as a word of warning to people who torment others to the extent that their victims feel that no one on earth can help them, and they turn to Hashem and beg Him to fight on their behalf.

I sincerely believe that the desperate prayers of suffering victims are a terrible accusation in Heaven. Hashem is Father to everyone, but especially to the downtrodden. The Merciful and Compassionate God sees when one of his creations is suffering terribly at the hands of another and hears pleas for help. Hashem is also a zealous and revengeful God who is liable to exact a terrible punishment in answer to these heartfelt *tefillos*.

Shortly after I finished high school I got married. My husband is a gentle, considerate and sensitive person, and with his love and understanding I was able to rebuild my emotional well-being. Some scars still remain, though, and probably will never fully heal.

I feel that I have bared my soul to you and your listeners. I know some people will laugh at me: "Does she really believe that tragedies befell people because of her?" Others may criticize me for having caused such tragedies. I can only say, "Do not judge your fellow man until you reach his situation," and I do not wish my situation at that time to befall anyone, ever.

"Open Your Eyes"

Dear Rabbi Walder,
My wife and I have a fixed routine on Sunday nights — we always listen to your radio program and to the letters you read from listeners. For a long time we have been asking ourselves whether we should send you our story too — and we have finally decided to do so.

I come from a totally secular Israeli home. By secular I mean atheist — we held no religious beliefs at all, and no Jewish traditions and practices were kept. Yom Kippur was ignored, and I didn't even celebrate my *bar mitzvah*.

When I was 16, I began to search for some kind of meaning to life, although at the time I didn't call it that since I didn't realize what I was doing. I liked rebels, and I started hanging out with all kinds of weird people. I dressed and acted like a kind of hippie, and caused no end of embarrassment to my parents. As I approached the age of 18, what hurt them most was that I did not want to serve in the Israeli army. Now, my parents may be atheists but their love for Eretz Yisrael and dedication to its defense was a religion in itself. I guess you could say that this was the one remnant of their Jewish beliefs, and they were devastated that I wouldn't want to be part of the Israel Defense Forces.

I, on the other hand, had gone farther than they had — nothing at all was sacred to me. I didn't believe in anything. Since the army was not any more interested in a weird character like me than I was in them, I was free to roam around the country with all the strange characters who were my friends. I could fill a book with my adventures from then.

At the age of 21, I packed my bags and set off for India — to look for truth! In my quest for meaning, there was no commune or ashram that I did not visit. I got to know many gurus personally. Only someone who has spent time in India can really understand the magnetic force of these communes.

You see, the average secular young person from the permissive and hedonistic culture of our day has already experienced a lot of the materialistic pleasures to be found in the world by the time he's 21. Some keep on searching for new experiences, but even they will despair after a few years. They don't have a higher purpose in life.

These young people have been "brainwashed" against their own traditions, and it doesn't enter their minds to search for the true meaning in life in "their own backyard" — in the eternal values of Judaism and living an observant Jewish life. They want to find something new — and they discover it in India.

It's true that India has a special power over anyone who visits. The people have a completely different outlook on life — they are never in a rush, nothing bothers them and they have answers for every question! I met some truly amazing people there, extremely spiritual people who were able to exercise total control over their lives. There were monks who led an ascetic life-style and fasted for long periods of time. One monk I met decided that if a serpent could hold its breath for many minutes, there was no reason why a human being couldn't do so and he spent his days doing breathing exercises, training himself to hold his breath for long periods of time. I was very impressed by their single-minded determination to achieve their aims. My generation is a spoiled one and never had to work hard for anything, so such purposefulness was new to me and it really amazed me.

Yet eventually I became disillusioned with their beliefs. An inner voice said, What's the purpose of all this? Even if I stand in awe of someone who has such self-control that he can hold his breath for a long time, or keep his hand in a certain position for hours on end, what's he doing it for? The more I admired their abilities, the more it bothered me that they seemed to be wasting those abilities on what for me were insignificant matters.

My roaming and searching continued and eventually I went to visit the Dalai Lama himself.

The Dalai Lama comes from Tibet. During the Chinese invasion and takeover of Tibet, the Dalai Lama's followers were able to smuggle him over the border to India where he has lived ever since.

He is one of the few leaders in the world who truly believes in non-violence, even for purposes of defense. As a result, the Tibetans no longer have a country of their own. Nevertheless the Dalai Lama is revered by all, and he received the Nobel Prize for peace in recognition of his unswerving quest for world peace.

I was captivated by the Dalai Lama's personality, by his wisdom and intelligence. I would rise early each morning and attend his daily sermon at 4:30 AM. As far as I was concerned, he was a human being without any blemishes.

Back home in Israel, my parents were worried about me. My father sent me a letter saying he had heard that I had "freaked out" — in other words, he was afraid that I'd really gone crazy. I sent a polite letter back assuring him that I wasn't crazy but that I was now at a major crossroads in my life. As I mailed the letter I realized that the very wording of my letter would convince my father that I had indeed gone crazy!

The same evening I approached one of the Dalai Lama's assistants and asked for a private audience with the Dalai Lama the next morning after his sermon.

The following morning I entered his chambers. He was a gentleman who greeted everyone who came to see him. He bowed to me and offered me a seat. My words poured forth, as I told him that I saw truth and meaning in his religion and that I had decided to adopt it if he would accept me.

"Where are you from," he asked me.

"Israel."

He looked at me. "Are you Jewish?"

"Yes!" I replied.

His reaction surprised me. His expression turned from friendly to puzzled — with even a tinge of anger. He told me that he did not understand my decision, and that he would not permit me to carry it out.

I was stunned. What did he mean?

"All religions are an imitation of Judaism," he stated. "I am sure that when you lived in Israel, your eyes were closed. Please take the first plane back to Israel and *open your eyes*. Why settle for an imitation when you can have the real thing?"

His words spun around in my head the whole day. I thought to myself: I am a Jew and an Israeli, but I know nothing about my own religion. Did I have to search and wander the whole world only to be told that I was blind and that the answers I was seeking were to be found on my own doorstep?

I did what the Dalai Lama told me to do. I immediately flew back to Israel — and entered a yeshivah! And, as he told me to do, I opened my eyes. I began to see that the Dalai Lama had indeed been correct. I discovered Judaism and its vitality, and that it encompassed everything in life. I embraced its laws and found many reasons to live — at least 613 reasons! And I found joy.

Two years later I was offered a *shidduch*. Anat was a young woman of my age who was also a *ba'alas teshuvah*. She too had been to Goa and other places in India to search for answers, and she too had found them back in Israel — in the religion of Israel. We clicked immediately. We had gone through the same process, and we had experienced the same doubts, the same despair from life, the same search for meaning, and the same return to our roots. After several dates, Anat and I got engaged.

When I went to pay the matchmaker, she refused to accept money, saying that she didn't deserve it.

"But it's customary to pay the matchmaker — and I want to do it."

"You are quite right, but in this case I am not the matchmaker," she replied simply.

"What do you mean?

"I'll tell you. Anat came to me and showed me a piece of paper with a name on it. She asked me to introduce her to the person whose name was written there. She knew nothing at all about that person, but said that she had been given his name by someone she trusts completely… It was your name."

After the engagement party, Anat and I went for a walk.

"Tell me," I said, "how did this *shidduch* come about? I want to know who gave you my name, so that I can pay him."

Anat smiled. "You will have to travel to India to pay him."

Before I had a chance to react, she continued, "I haven't told you yet that at the end of my wandering, I went to the Dalai Lama. I was very impressed by him and all he embodied and I decided to join his religion. When I told him that he said, 'Anat, since you are Jewish you should not settle for silver if you can have gold.' He told me to return to my roots and then in a whisper, he asked one of his assistants to bring him a piece of paper. The Dalai Lama then copied the name that was there onto another piece of paper, and handed it to me. 'This is your soulmate,' he told me.

"When I returned to Israel, I joined a seminary for *ba'alos teshuvah*, and I saw the light. And you know the rest. You know, at first it was because of the Dalai Lama, and only later the much stronger light of Judaism attracted me. And only after a year had gone by did I begin to search for you. I approached many *shadchanim*, but no one was able to discover you in the various yeshivos for *ba'alei teshuvah*. Then someone contacted yours, and — I found you!

"From the very first date I knew that the Dalai Lama was right."

Anat and I have been married for three years now and we have been blessed with two wonderful children. I am immersed in Torah study, and Anat is a wonderful wife and mother. And our parents, you may be wondering — how did they accept all this? Our parents are educated, well-to-do people whose way of life is very different from ours — but they are impressed by our lifestyle and the close relationship between us. They know the role of the Dalai Lama in all this and have told the story to their friends. It's not a story you hear every day!

Living a Lie

D ear Rabbi Walder,
   I am a 14-year-old girl in eighth grade. I know that most of the letters you read on your program are from adults, but I hope that you will still take note of mine.

Let me introduce myself to you. My name is Miriam, and I am an ordinary girl. I have lots of friends, and I like school. I do well in my studies. I have never had any problems with my teachers and friends, and certainly not within my family. I come from a warm and loving family. I have wonderful parents whom I love dearly. People say that I am smart — I don't think I'm smarter than any other girl my age, but it's true that I think a lot, probably more than most other girls my age. As a result of all my reflections, I am quite serious, maybe too much so.

The last two weeks have seen a lot of action in my eighth grade class. You can imagine why — high schools.

Rabbi Walder, I know that you once wrote an article on this issue and it generated a lot of discussion among people. Now the girls in my class can talk of nothing else: "Which schools did you apply to? Where were you accepted? Have you got a place for next year already?"

Most girls I know get accepted to the school of their choice, and other girls might not get into their first choice of school but at least they have a place. And then there are the unfortunate girls who don't get accepted *anywhere* they have applied to.

They walk around dejectedly, gazing enviously at their classmates who already have a place for next year and are busily planning. These poor girls have nothing to look forward to and nothing to talk about. Well, in fact they do have a lot to say, about how their parents are trying to exert pressure and use any influence they have to try and get their daughters accepted into a good high school. As each day passes and they have still not received a positive reply, their faces look gloomier and more despairing.

I am among those happy girls sitting with friends and working things out for next year. I've already planned who I will sit next to in class, we've taken bets as to who our teacher will be, and we've assured each other that even if we are put in different classes, we'll still keep in touch.

Whenever I catch sight of the jealous looks from the other girls, my heart fills with sorrow. I know how sad they are. They feel full of despair and fear. Yes, they are frightened. You described the feelings so well in your article, Rabbi Walder. These girls fear that all their friends are embarking on a new journey and only they are left behind.

Rabbi Walder, I am about to reveal a secret to you. None of my classmates are aware of my secret. The truth is that I also was not accepted to any high school of my choice. I am living a lie, not giving anyone the slightest hint of the truth. Half my friends are happy for me and with me, the other half are full of jealousy and I am alone, unable to share the terrible truth with anyone.

I know what I mean when I say terrible. My older sister went through the same ordeal. She too was not accepted to any of the high schools of her choice, and she ended up studying at a school which was not right for her, where the girls and the studies were way below her level. The experience was terrible for her and her self-image really suffered. She married as soon as she could — I think it was her way of running away from her troubles. However, she just went from "the frying pan into the fire." When I look at my beloved sister now, I remember her as she was — smart and full of zest for life (just as I am now). I can't bear to see what happened to her because she was forced to leave her natural surroundings and her good friends and go to a school below her level in every way.

All of this had nothing to do with *her* as an individual. She was not at fault, and nor am I to blame that we were not accepted to good high schools. Both of us are good girls who never had any problems in school with our studies or our behavior, nor was there a problem of not dressing modestly, or anything like that.

The "problem" has something to do with one of our parents. Rabbi Walder, I would dearly love to tell you the exact details so you could see for yourself that it is a petty, insignificant problem but I have decided not to tell you because I am afraid that someone will identify me as the writer, even though this "problem" can be found in hundreds of families.

As you can imagine, my parents are trying every possible way and are pulling every possible string to try and get me accepted to a school that is right for me. However, since they are not considered important people, they won't get very far. No one wants to speak to them or help them. When you are considered a nobody, an insignificant number, then your plight does not interest anyone. Of course the powers-that-be will give very convincing reasons why they cannot accept me and for a period of time we might actually believe that they are sincere in their refusal. At the same time, I feel that some hidden power is taking me out of my natural milieu, distancing me from my friends and forcing me to leave my life behind. I am so saddened by all of this, yet I do not cry. It's still too early and I don't want to cause distress to my parents, after all they suffered with my sister. Now they, and I, are fearful of what will happen to me. Their instincts are correct — they have every reason to view my future with trepidation.

I only have to look at my sister to know what awaits me. And I am not prepared to suffer as she has. Period. It may sound awful to say this, but I don't possess the inner strength to endure what she did.

Elementary school is out for the summer in one month. I have one more month left of fun with my friends. We will make plans for next year and then we will be on summer vacation. I will probably go to camp and have a wonderful time singing, playing and living a carefree existence. Then the first week of September will arrive. I don't yet know what I plan to do then but I have time to decide. I have plenty of ideas and plans but one thing is clear. I do not intend to suffer like my sister.

Rabbi Walder, please listen to me and understand what I am shouting: I don't have the strength! I am crying as I write this. I am including a poem I wrote describing my feelings. If you feel it is appropriate, please read it aloud:

*Enough of my tears have fallen — you don't need to cry
    for me.*
*The streets are drenched with mine — you don't need to
    lie for me.*
*Just carry on with your lives, don't spare a thought for
    mine.*
*I have stepped out of your lives, I won't take more of your
    time.*
*There's one thing I have learned — it's not enough to
    plant a tree.*
You must tend it, stake it, water it — it's a necessity.

I'm nothing but a small plant, about to be uprooted,
Blowing in the wind, forgotten and unsuited.
Unwanted and unnoticed, doomed to the worst.
But I will ask: Have you forgotten the King of the
*   Universe??*
To whom do all the plants belong, and everything in
*   creation?*
And friendship and responsibility among the Jewish
*   nation?*
Can anybody help me? I ask as I cry.
Through my tears I will await your reply.

Where Are You, Hannah?

Dear Rabbi Walder,

I am a 32-year-old happily married man. The story I am going to tell you took place some years ago when I was a *yeshivah bachur* going out on *shidduchim*. I studied at a well-known yeshivah where I was considered a popular and learned student, and I had no shortage of excellent suggestions from matchmakers. Many girls from good families, families who would support my Torah study, were proposed — all I had to do was say "yes." But that was my problem — with all those suggestions, I couldn't make up my mind! Word got around that I was picky and fussy, that I would go out with a girl only once, and then go on to the next one. Although I didn't consider myself to be choosy, the truth is that I did go out with a lot of girls. In order to avoid unpleasant situations, I made it a rule never to meet a girl for the first time at her home, so that I would not have to give a negative answer after already having met the parents. If things went well during the first meeting, then I would agree to meet a girl for a second time in her house.

It was thanks to this rule that I am writing you my story.

A girl was suggested for me, and my parents made the usual inquiries. She sounded like an excellent girl and everything about her and her background seemed just right. I arranged to meet her, as usual, at one of the popular venues for such dates, in our circle — the lobby of one of Jerusalem's large hotels.

When I arrived, I saw a girl sitting and waiting, so I asked her if she was Hannah. She smiled and answered in the affirmative, and I sat down.

We began to talk. Everything seemed to fit perfectly. We held the same opinions on many issues and the conversation flowed freely. It only took 10 minutes for me to decide that I wanted to continue to date her. We were so engrossed in our conversation that it took some time until we noticed a young man sitting at a table near us. He was fidgeting nervously in his seat, obviously waiting for his date to show up. He ordered a drink and was constantly looking around for someone to come. Out of the corner of my eye, I noticed a young girl sitting in the far corner of the lobby, and she was also quite obviously waiting for her date to appear. At some point, the young man seated near us went over to the girl, asked her a question and then walked out of the hotel. She hung around waiting for some time, and then out of despair she also walked out.

Hannah and I sat talking for more than three hours, which is far longer than is customary for a first date. As we got up to leave, I told her that I would be very happy to see her again and she agreed. We agreed that the matchmaker would coordinate the day, as is done in our circles, and that we would meet at her parents' house. I saw her into a cab, and then I made my own way home.

I barely had a chance to get through the front door when my parents jumped on me: "Shlomo! What's going on? Where have you been? We've been so worried!"

"What do you mean?" I asked. "I've been out on the *shidduch*, as we arrranged."

"So why did the girl return home and tell her parents that you didn't turn up?"

"What do you mean? I've just spent the last three hours in her company!"

I asked my parents to call up the girl's family so that I could speak to her. As soon as I heard her voice on the telephone, I realized what had happened: The girl I had spent a wonderful evening with was not the one I had arranged to meet! I asked her if she had sat and waited for me in the far corner of the lobby and if at some point a *yeshivah bachur* had approached her. She replied that a young man had indeed come up to her and asked if she was the girl he was waiting for!

I then asked her if she had noticed a couple sitting next to the central pillar of the lobby. When she said yes, I explained to her what had happened and apologized profusely for having caused her so much distress. I told her that I would discuss the matter with my parents and we would be in contact with the *shadchanis*.

My parents found the incident amusing, but then they became serious and asked me when I was going to meet the girl I had originally intended to.

"The truth is," I replied, "that I don't want to meet anybody else. I want to arrange another date with the girl I met this evening."

"But who is she?"

"Hannah!"

"Hannah who? Where does she live? Who are her parents?"

As I made a mental summary of the evening's conversation, I realized that although we had spent the entire evening talking, I didn't know the first thing about Hannah — not her family name, address, school, or anything at all besides her first name.

The next day I contacted all the matchmakers I knew, and

asked them if they knew of a Hannah whose intended date had not turned up for the meeting. It was all to no avail — no one knew anything about Hannah.

When my parents saw that I was making no progress, they suggested again that I meet the original girl who had been suggested.

I shook my head. "I'm sorry, but I must find Hannah. I know she's out there somewhere waiting for me, and I have to find her."

Weeks passed, months passed, and seeds of doubt began to grow in my mind — maybe I would never find her. Maybe she wasn't interested in meeting me again anyway. But whenever I thought about her, and the fact that I might never meet her again, I felt a great pain in my heart. This gave me the strength to continue my search, for I knew my heart was letting me know that she was my *bashert*, my intended, the girl I had been waiting for all this time.

When a year had passed, I realized I had no choice but to abandon my futile search and re-enter the *shidduch* scene. This was no simple matter, as I discovered that I could not get Hannah out of my mind.

Another year passed, and a certain *shadchanis* summed up my situation bluntly: "Shlomo, you have no right meeting a girl and raising her hopes when you know full well that nothing will come of it." She was right! My heart belonged to a girl whom I had met two years ago for one evening, and who might even have gotten married in the meantime.

Rabbi Walder, it is too painful to try to describe the next five years of my life; let me just say that I became a sad, lonely *alte bachur*.

One day, my mother received a phone call from a *shadchanis* she did not know. Mrs. Cohen said she had a really special girl to offer me.

"Please let me know her name so I can make my own inquiries," my mother said, which was her standard reply to all suggestions.

When my mother heard the family name, she replied, "I'm sorry, but we are not interested in this *shidduch*. We are an Ashkenazic family and my son will not marry a Sephardic girl." My mother was polite but firm. When she told me about this suggestion later, I accepted her answer because that is how I had been brought up. (It may sound strange to someone not in our circles, but Ashkenazim and Sephardim generally didn't date each other. It was felt that customs, traditions, and general background in a *shidduch* had to match.)

Mrs. Cohen continued to contact my mother with other suggestions for me, but since they were all Sephardic girls my mother would not consider them. I couldn't understand why Mrs. Cohen didn't get the message and give up, but it turned out that she was a very warm and concerned woman who was absolutely dedicated to making matches. My mother eventually found herself pouring out her woes about me, and she mentioned my encounter with Hannah years before. Mrs. Cohen offered to help, but my mother told her that we had explored every possible avenue without success.

One evening the phone rang, and it was Mrs. Cohen. I could hear her voice from the other side of the room: *"I've found her!"*

When she had first heard my story she'd contacted her network of *shadchanim*. It took her more than ten phone calls, but she finally was given the number of a woman who confirmed that her daughter had indeed mistakenly met a certain boy several years earlier and then all contact was lost. It emerged that her daughter, like me, had spent those years convinced she had met her *bashert* and hoping she would find him again.

I grabbed the phone from my mother and asked Mrs. Cohen to please set up a meeting between me and Hannah as soon as possible.

"Um, I'm afraid there's one slight problem, Shlomo."

"Don't tell me she's married!"

"No, no — that's not the problem — it's just that she is from a 100% pure Sephardic family. I don't think your mother will want you to meet her."

"Mrs. Cohen," I replied happily, "That's irrelevant. This is the right girl for me!"

I waited for my parents' opposition, but I was pleasantly surprised that there was none.

Within a few days we met. I recognized her immediately, but the funny thing was that she wasn't called Hannah. At our first meeting she had just smiled politely when I asked her if she was Hannah. She hadn't heard what I'd said, since it seemed obvious to her that I was her date, and I'd thought she said yes. Well, we spent the entire evening recounting the efforts we had each made to meet again. Suddenly the full consequence of my narrow-mindedness hit me. The reason I had been unable to find her was that it hadn't even occurred to me that the girl I was searching for could be Sephardic — and so I hadn't approached a single Sephardic matchmaker!

We got engaged after a few meetings, and both families were very happy.

Rabbi Walder, we have been happily married for several years now, and I have thought a lot about people's prejudices. Who knows how much happiness we deny ourselves because of preconceived ideas and unfounded beliefs. Take my story, for example — my wife and I would never have met under normal circumstances because of our "different backgrounds." But since we met under "false pretenses" — that is, without any preconceived ideas — we were able to appreciate each other's worth as human beings.

There are probably hundreds, if not thousands, of single people out there who are still single because of their and their families' old-fashioned, unfounded beliefs. Why do we Jews always have to compartmentalize ourselves into many sub-divisions — Sephardim and Ashkenazim, Chasidim and Litvaks, etc., when we are all brothers?

Hashem looks down on us, His People, and only He knows what we are missing out on. I, for one, only have to take one look at my beloved wife and our wonderful children to know what I could have missed out on.

PENITENTiary

Dear Rabbi Walder,

My story is not an unusual one. I grew up in a simple, traditional family in Tel Aviv. The street had more influence on me than my parents did, and by the time I was 21, although I still wore a yarmulke, it was more out of habit than any beliefs. I kept Shabbos in public, but otherwise I led a secular life.

I married my high-school girlfriend, Miri, and held a variety of jobs, but none of them were very steady. Within a few years I was hanging around with my buddies and neglecting my wife and children. My poor wife was left alone to raise the children and support the family. And I? I came and went as I pleased, and if she dared make a comment about my behavior I would explode in a fit of anger and accuse her of depriving me of my freedom.

I admit I was very juvenile about my "independence." I would flare up whenever anyone commented that I ought to be doing anything other than what I was doing, be it an employer, neighbor, or relative. After a while people became accustomed to leaving me alone. I felt great, that I'd succeeded in making it clear to everyone that they should stop minding my business. I thought this meant that other people respected me, but I didn't realize that they just stayed out of my way because of my temper! Looking back, I see I was no more than a wild animal. I was living a life devoid of expectation, obligation, rules or limitations.

About six years ago I got involved in a brawl at the local open-air market. I was not directly involved when the fight began, but with my red-hot temper I quickly joined in as if I were personally affected by the argument. By the time it was all over, two of the participants were taken away — one by ambulance, and one — me — by police car.

The trial date was set, and I didn't take the whole matter seriously. After all, I was forever getting into fights, and I didn't think that one more brawl meant anything.

The day of the trial came, and as I sat in the dock, it dawned on me that this time I was in big trouble. I was accused of being directly responsible for the assault. The other fellow's lawyers described me as a violent person, and brought witnesses to testify against me. The lawyers also presented photographs of the plaintiff's injuries, and even I admit that they did not look pretty.

My lawyer was quite open with me and told me to expect the worst. He presented a plea bargain where I admitted my guilt and received a sentence of two-and-a-half years. My wife and children sat in the courtroom crying, and I felt that I had reached the lowest point in my life.

I had always considered myself to be basically a good guy who stayed out of trouble, and now I found myself branded a criminal, handcuffed, and put behind bars.

I shared a crowded cell with 12 other hardened criminals. Within days I was deeply depressed. Life in prison was like being on a different planet. Here the law of the jungle ruled. You could be a powerful millionaire on the "outside," but here, on the "inside," the garbage collector could be more respected than you. The cardinal rule was to never display any sign of weakness — that would finish you.

At the beginning I sat in the corner of the cell quite oblivious to my surroundings, wallowing in self-pity. The other inmates did not dare start up with me, since they knew I had been sent here for grievous bodily assault. Outside the prison walls, that is considered a crime, but on the inside, it makes you important. After brooding in my corner several days, someone gave me a piece of advice: "Hey, snap out of it, will you? Otherwise your fellow inmates are not going to think too highly of you." And that is not advisable within the prison walls!

So I acted like a hardened criminal, but deep down I felt as if I were dying. I had always valued my freedom above every-thing else, and here I was locked up with murderers and thieves and the rest, deprived of my liberty. A man can easily lose his human dignity in prison. I sank into a deep depression, I lost my appetite, and yearned for my wife and children. The worst was that I cried myself to sleep at night. Anyone who knows any-thing about prison life knows that a prisoner caught crying is doomed to suffer terribly because of his "weakness."

I can tell you that I encountered the full range of abuse — physical, verbal, and mental — and it was only after I assaulted Jackie, my chief tormentor, that I earned of bit of respite. Of course assaulting a fellow prisoner is a serious crime according to the authorities and I was liable to have my sentence ex-tended, but the unwritten law between prisoners says never, never to tell on your fellow inmates. So Jackie innocently told the doctor at the prison infirmary that he had fallen out of bed. Of course no one believed him, because he was black and blue all over and it looked more likely that he had fallen off a sky-scraper and landed on a pile of broken glass! The authorities knew full well that I was the culprit, but since Jackie would not admit anything they had no case against me. However, the chief warden called me over and warned me that they would be watching me like a hawk, and if there was the slightest bit of trouble, they would recommend against reducing my sentence as a result of good behavior. I realized that they had the power to keep me in this place for many years.

Although my status among my fellow inmates had improved greatly, I was heading for a nervous breakdown. I had never had a particularly strong character, and now I felt that I was falling into a bottomless pit, spinning out of control.

I decided to take stock of my life. A visit from my wife and eldest daughter was a breaking point for me; I felt so worthless sitting there in front of them, and I saw that my wife was suffering terribly. I knew that if I sat there one more minute I would break down and cry like a child. So I got up and walked away, 20 minutes before the visit was officially over, leaving them both in tears. The wardens couldn't believe how "heartless" I was. I sent my wife a message telling her not to come again, that their visits were too painful for me.

I became an introvert. I tried to figure out how I had fallen so low. Slowly but surely I turned to religion, to the life that I was born into but that I'd rejected without a thought. I began to pray three times a day, and say the Grace after Meals. I even started to attend the *shiurim* arranged by the prison rabbi.

When he suggested that I transfer to the special wing reserved for Orthodox prisoners, I insisted on staying where I was. I wanted to become a *ba'al teshuvah* in my natural milieu. At first, my fellow inmates thought I was just putting on a show, but they gradually realized that I was serious.

I was determined to start a new life. Rabbi Turgeman from Bnei Brak was a regular visitor at the prison, and I spent many hours in conversation with him. One of the many words of wisdom he imparted to me was that it was not enough to work only on my relationship with Hashem; I would have to work on improving my relationship with my fellowmen. He suggested that

I begin by making a point of helping other prisoners whenever I could, to overcome my negative traits and learn to become considerate of others. I also had to start to work on controlling my temper. As far as I was concerned, praying three times a day was much easier than dealing with people, because no one disturbed me during my prayers. Rabbi Turgeman tried to show me the importance of putting my fellowman's needs before my own. This sounded easy in theory, but in practice it was much harder than sitting in front of a Gemara and studying.

Rabbi Turgeman suggested that an important step would be to apologize to Jackie. I tried to explain to Rabbi Turgeman that he had been tormenting me continuously, and I'd had to fight him to save my life! He saw my point, but claimed that since I had proved my strength to Jackie, I had nothing to lose by apologizing to him. I told Rabbi Turgeman that among prison inmates there is an unwritten rule never to apologize. An apology is interpreted as a sign of weakness or as a meaningless act which is only done out of fear of reprisal. Rabbi Turgeman listened sympathetically but he said that I was just looking for excuses to avoid having to take this difficult but important step. He asked me if I simply wanted to conquer my weak points or if I felt it was necessary to fight the whole world. "Just go ahead and apologize to Jackie!" he said, giving me a friendly pat on the back and a wink of encouragement.

Today, when I look back at the incident, it seems so trivial, but then it was the most significant act I had ever undertaken.

The next day, in the dining room, in the middle of lunch, I stood up called for quiet. In front of the entire prison population I apologized to Jackie. Stunned silence greeted my apology. Nothing like this had ever happened in prison! Then, spontaneously, they all started cheering us on and led Jackie and me to the center of the dining hall and we shook hands. I was surprised that I had emerged as a "winner," that they hadn't interpreted the apology as a sign of weakness.

Once I had overcome the hurdle of working on my pride, everything else came much easier. It's like mountain climbing — they say the first peak is always the hardest, but once that challenge has been met, you feel ready to climb any mountain in the world.

My next project was to work on my relationship with my fellow inmates. I tried to greet everyone with a smile, to let others in front of me in a line, to share jobs, and most of all to encourage people. Before I realized it, I had become a popular and respected man — an entirely new reality for me. I was invited to settle arguments between prisoners and I always tried to reach a compromise so that the loser would not be insulted. Slowly but surely, more prisoners became attracted to my way of life and they also became *ba'alei teshuvah*. It was a snowball effect — they saw the positive changes in my life and how my belief in Hashem had changed me for the better, so they wanted this for themselves too. We made strange bedfellows but due to our common beliefs we became a close-knit group devoted to each other.

We now had a large *minyan* three times a day, and under the circumstances, I felt that life in prison was treating me well.

Shortly afterwards I was informed that I was to be released early on account of good behavior. I hadn't realized how time had flown by so fast. My fellow inmates were really happy for me — they organized parties and showered me with love and warmth. On my last night in prison we sat together singing. We hugged each other and shed a few tears as well. A lot of my friends expressed worry over what would become of them without having me as their leader, and I promised to keep in touch. The hardest part was saying good-bye to Jackie, who had become my best friend. Our fight and reconciliation had been a turning point in both our lives.

The following morning I left the prison gates behind me and headed for home. My wife got a shock when she saw my beard and yarmulke — I think she was afraid that I'd gone crazy. Soon enough, though, she noticed the positive changes in me. I began to work for a printer, and at the end of my work day I come straight home. In the evenings I often study in the local *kollel*.

My wild outbursts are now a thing of the past and I make it a point to speak calmly. My family, who suffered so much on my account, are now able to get *nachas* from me.

A year later, Jackie was released, and I was there to greet him when he left the prison. I made sure that he went into a rehabilitation program, and I helped him with his adjustment to regular life. He became a *ba'al teshuvah* and married a wonderful woman. We sometimes study together in *kollel*.

I am now a happily married man with six children. Hashem has given me many blessings, and I look back to the time I spent behind bars as one of the best times of my life — even though in some ways it was the worst. I underwent a cleansing process in prison. I entered as a wild animal and left as a decent human being and Jew. I entered as an idle good-for-nothing and left as a busy person who was looked up to as a leader.

Rabbi Walder, I will end my story with one of the morning blessings that I say every day with great feeling: "Blessed are You, Hashem, Who releases prisoners." I thank God for sending me to prison — and for releasing me.

Listen to Me!

Dear Rabbi Walder,

    I don't know if you will be pleased to receive this letter. Believe me, it took me a long time to work up the courage to write it.

I am 15 years old, the firstborn child in my family. My parents are much younger than most of my friends' parents and they are really friendly and open people. I had a great childhood and have only fond memories of those years, especially of my father, who always found time to play with me. I knew he was always there for me if I had a problem.

All that changed as I entered my teens. As you know, Rabbi Walder, teenagers often have problems dealing with themselves and so did I, but my parents didn't seem to notice. I felt that they were distancing themselves from me somehow.

One problem was my younger sister, Suri. In my parents' eyes Suri could do no wrong. She was always asking my Mom what she could do to help in the house, whereas they had to ask me two or three times to do things. Well, it didn't take long for Suri to become known as the "little balabuste" and me to be labeled "lazy." In my opinion, my parents should have taken me aside and gently explained how they expected me to help around the house. I'm sure that if they had given me support and encouragement, I would have willingly helped, but they didn't. My parents considered me to be lazy and did nothing to encourage me to change my ways, so I just carried on fulfilling their low expectations.

My smart parents, who both work in education, broke *every* rule in the book. They were forever comparing Suri and me, even in public. They would praise Suri for her diligence and criticize me for my laziness. You can imagine how I felt, but what really hurt me was their insensitivity. Couldn't they see what damage they were doing?

Of course, there were times when I pitched in and worked like a slave around the house. When my mother was in the hospital, Suri and I worked together as a team to run the house. But when my mother came home she noticed only what Suri had done, and told her friends how she couldn't have managed without Suri. I now realized, more than *ever*, that I didn't mean anything to them.

Actually, my relationship with my mother has never been great. She wanted to be both my mother and my friend, but when she realized that she couldn't be both, I guess she decided to be neither — neither friend nor mother. My father had always been my number-1 fan. He always said I had my head firmly placed on my shoulders. Even now he still compliments me on my brains, but I suspect he just wants to prove to me (and himself) that he has nothing against me. I can see through him, though, and I know that he still prefers Suri's easygoing personality to my brains. They don't lose any sleep over her!

I have analyzed my predicament and reached the conclusion that my parents only care about their peace and quiet, not about the consequences of their behavior. They don't want to deal with the fact that I, their oldest daughter, who could give them such *nachas*, desperately needs their love and support.

But no — it is much easier for them to enjoy their mediocre daughter, Suri, who automatically does what she is told. Don't get me wrong, I have nothing against Suri's ordinariness. I am just bitter that she is so important to my parents and I seem to be a mere object in their eyes.

I haven't mentioned my brother, Moshe, who is between Suri and me. He is certainly no angel — he doesn't help at home, and even worse, he's a poor student. But the contrast in the way they deal with him as opposed to me is very strong. They treat him with kid gloves, respect him, and give him the honor befitting an only son. I know that they are aware of all his shortcomings, but they keep silent. I guess they're frightened of him or of how he might react if they try to tackle his behavior. I simply don't understand them.

Don't they realize that I have a big problem? I am desperate for help.

I admit I'm not perfect. Everyone has faults and I *should* help more at home. By nature, I'm a thinker, not a doer. But the way my parents deal with me is to pretend I don't exist. They put all their energy into Suri. They probably don't think that I desperately need their approval because I give the impression of being strong, even a bit sarcastic sometimes. But if only they knew how I really felt, how I am shattered and suffering, how I hate the whole world sometimes. I often think about running away — but where? I don't have any answers.

Why, oh why can't my parents see my desperation? At one point I thought that maybe it was my fault, that I was not communicating well with them. So I spoke to a teacher at school whom I'm close to, and asked her to try and speak to them. She did, and my parents reassured her that I was just "going through a phase" and it would soon pass. Since then I haven't heard the end of it — they are forever making nasty remarks about their daughter who has to turn to outsiders for help. What do they think I am, a little crybaby!?

Rabbi Walder, this is what I'd like to say to my parents:

Dear Mom and Dad (you see, deep down I do love them),
Please, please stop what you are doing to me. Don't ignore me, don't insult me, stop your snide remarks, don't favor Suri over me. Please, please acknowledge me, notice my despair, understand how difficult it is to be a teenager. Show me that you love me and care about me. Please, please, I beg of you.
Mom and Dad, listen to your own daughter! We live in the same house — can't you see I am crying and suffering?

Horse Sense

Dear Rabbi Walder,

My friends convinced me to write to you — and it's true I have a lot to say.

I come from a troubled neighborhood rife with crime and drugs. Some of the people I grew up with are no longer alive — and believe me, they didn't die of natural causes at a ripe old age! I spent my youth hanging out with a bad crowd and I drifted into the crime scene. I was considered a wild and unruly kid who had no respect for anyone or anything. People kept out of my way and everyone was wary of me.

It wasn't long before I was into drugs in a big way. I would do anything for a few dollars so that I could get my daily fix — even cheat my parents. By then I had no self-respect left, and there were many days I felt so worthless and empty that I just wished I would die.

Then, one day I'd had enough. I couldn't go on like that another day. I decided to come clean. I don't know where I got the strength, but I proved everyone wrong and I kicked my drug habit. Even the local police, who knew me well, couldn't believe that I was serious. They were sure that sooner or later I would slip back into my old ways. Whenever there was a break-in in the neighborhood, they would arrest me for questioning. Eventually, though, they realized that I was serious and they left me alone.

I started to look for work, but I quickly discovered that no one wants to employ former drug addicts. One employer told me, "Once a drug addict, always a drug addict." This was my fear, actually — that the minute I thought "It won't happen to me again," I'd slip back into my old ways. I did manage to find work here and there, but the minute anything was missing, or another employee couldn't find a particular item, then all eyes turned on me. I was always guilty in others' eyes and eventually dismissed from my jobs. No one wanted to believe that a criminal could really turn over a new leaf.

Being unemployed was a very dangerous situation for me, and I feared it was only a matter of time before I slipped back into my bad old ways.

One day I met a friend, Chaim, who suggested I work with him in setting up a stable. I didn't have the faintest idea why he was interested in horses, but since I wasn't doing much else I decided to work with him. We got to work building stables and a fence around the plot of land, and then Chaim brought in the horses. We worked around the clock for a month, and by the time we had finished, our place really looked great, if I do say so myself. I didn't earn anything but at least I was off the streets and had something to do.

Pretty soon, the local kids started dropping by and we greeted them warmly and let them have a ride on the horses. The police did not take kindly to all this — they were convinced that the stable was just a front for something criminal. They harassed us and tried to warn the kids to keep away from "dangerous" types like us. Although I resented what the police were doing to us, I understood their motives. If I looked at it from their point of view, neither Chaim nor I had a clean record and they had a certain justification in being suspicious about our activities. We had no choice but to turn the children away so that the cops would leave us alone, but there was one particular boy, Yossi, who persistently came back, no matter how many times we sent him away.

Yossi was twelve years old, and came from a troubled family. Looking at him you could see he was starved for love — and to tell you the truth, it was like looking at myself at that age. His young and tender soul had witnessed too much at home.

Whenever he came to our stable, he would do a great job taking care of the horses. Judging by the look on his face, you could see that this was the only place he found any measure of happiness. I grew closer to Yossi, and I began to tell him about my family history and the difficulties I had been through. When I saw that he wanted to hear from me about myself, I made a deal with him: He could only come and talk to me at the stable if he attended school on that day. I didn't want him to have the same memories that I have from school — I turned up for school for the first and last days of the school year!

As the weeks passed, Yossi began to look up to me as if I were his father. And he listened to what I had to say — which was more than you could say about his own father. His parents did not take kindly to this relationship, and they alerted the local social worker. I was warned not to have any more contact with Yossi.

When I informed Yossi of this latest development, he couldn't understand why his parents had done this. I actually understood why his parents were concerned, though, about their son spending so much time with someone like me! I always try to judge a matter from the other side's point of view. All Yossi would tell them was, "Let me go back to the stable, that's where I want to be!"

The following week, the social worker paid a visit to our stable. I tried to make a good impression on her, using long, high-falutin' words to describe what we do. But Chaim was in a bad mood and didn't try to make a good impression. He didn't know who Dina was, and didn't notice the looks I was trying to give him.

When she left, I was sure she was happy to be leaving such a place and people like us. But to my surprise, she wrote a very positive report about her visit. Her recommendation was to allow Yossi to return to the stable, as long as she could see that he wasn't picking up negative behavior from Chaim and me.

Yossi started to visit us again and I told him he would only be allowed to continue if he did well in school and wasn't influenced by the wrong kind of friends. Yossi kept to the rules — maybe only to please me, but still he did it. During the course of the year, other kids started coming by. These were boys who had dropped out of school and were in danger of ending up on the streets and getting involved in crime. They would come to our stable and help out with the horses and occasionally go riding with them.

Then, out of the blue, disaster struck. Our stable was declared an illegal construction, and three large tractors, accompanied by the police, drove up and destroyed the whole place. Within hours there was no trace left. All the time, effort, and love we had invested was gone. The police led the horses away to waiting trucks and drove off without saying a word.

The scene was too painful to bear, and I broke down and cried like a small child. Yossi and the other kids joined me and we sat on the ground crying as if it were Tisha b'Av! Now don't misunderstand me, Rabbi Walder, I'm not comparing our loss with the tragedy that befell the Jewish people at the time of the destruction of the Temple! But for Chaim and me and all our young friends, our world had fallen apart. Some time later, I noticed a distinguished looking man observing us. He started asking questions about the stable but we were glum and unfriendly, and just told him to go away. We tended to be suspicious of educated, well-dressed strangers. In his gentle but persistent voice, however, the visitor continued with his questions. He wanted to know why the youngsters liked coming to the stable, and what, in our opinion, it gave them. It was difficult for the kids to express themselves, but one thing came through: the boys told him that the only love and warmth they ever got was at our stable. The man listened attentively and when he got up to leave, he asked for my phone number.

A week later, a secretary from City Hall called to invite me to a meeting. She asked me to bring along three representatives of the youngsters who used to come to the stable. I arrived wearing my best clothes, and sat down at a table together with a group of psychologists and social workers. The man who had visited the stable after it had been destroyed — who was called Mr. Kraus — chaired the meeting. Everyone wanted to know about the stable and what we did with the youngsters who came to visit. I let the kids do most of the talking, and I admit that I felt my cheeks burn with embarrassment as Yossi and his friends praised me for the care and devotion I showered on them. No one had ever spoken so positively about me — not my parents and certainly not my teachers. I noticed that everyone present in the room was moved by the boys' words. Then Mr. Kraus closed the meeting and said that I would be invited back for a follow-up meeting.

Three days later I met with Mr. Kraus and two social workers. They wanted me to set up a "pilot program." They were prepared to rebuild the stable so that I could continue working with the youngsters, and they were prepared to refer other troubled children to me.

"Hold on, Mr. Kraus," I said. "I'm not some kind of agency you refer kids to! Anyone who wants to come is welcome, but they have to stick to the rules I set, and if I see that they don't fit in, then I won't want them to come back. In plain talk, I am the boss at the stable and I run it according to my own rules."

I went on to inform Mr. Kraus that although I was not a professional, life had been my best teacher and I knew what these kids were going through. And I knew I could help them. They trust me as one of them, I said, and not like the "trained professionals" who have no first-hand experience of the rough side of life. (Of course, I apologized to them for my blunt words.)

Mr. Kraus asked me to leave the room for a few minutes while they discussed my response to their offer. A few minutes later I was called back. Mr. Kraus said that they had agreed to my terms. They would rebuild the stable and I would be responsible for running it! I left the room overcome with happiness, but still not quite believing that it would actually happen. (I learned that Mr. Kraus is the Deputy Mayor. I only wish that all leaders were like him — he doesn't look down on anyone and respects what everyone has to say.)

True to his word, Mr. Kraus arranged for the stable to be rebuilt, and the new stable was far better than the first one. At first my relationship with Mr. Kraus and the social workers was rather cool, but gradually I came to realize that we all had the same goal: helping the troubled kids. Yossi came back to us, and today he is a serious young man who learns at a well-known yeshivah. He is like a son to me and he looks up to me as if I were his father. In the last four years, some 20 youngsters have been under my charge at the stable and the vast majority have turned out to be decent young men.

These years have changed my attitude to life entirely. I am now a qualified counselor dealing with street kids. I no longer ridicule education, and I have begun to study educational psychology. At first I couldn't believe I was actually studying all this theory, but I came to realize it all makes a lot of sense! I am often called to the municipal meetings on education to discuss problem teenagers and I always get a kick out of the fact that these highly educated professionals value my opinion!

Rabbi Walder, in many of your programs you talk about

troubled teenagers who hang around the streets. If only they had someone to talk to, someone they could really trust, then I'm sure they could be helped. It's not enough to send them to meet a psychologist in an office.

I want to end my letter by publicly thanking Mr. Kraus. He believed in me and trusted me to work with these troubled youngsters. Thanks to him I am what I am today. I pray that Hashem bless him with a long and healthy life.

Beaten

Dear Rabbi Walder,

I have been a fan of your show since it started. I couldn't make up my mind whether to write to you or not, but I finally decided that I had no choice — someone has to give me advice.

My story actually has two chapters which are, to my great sorrow, intertwined. I am now sixteen years old and the first chapter took place six years ago. I was a normal ten-year-old boy, but you might say that I was quite shy. I never had any problems at home or in school — I was not a star pupil or the most popular boy in class, but I was happy.

One summer afternoon I was riding around on my bike in the neighborhood. Although I usually rode together with my friends, on this particular day I was alone. One of my favorite places for riding was on the site of a factory which had closed down. I enjoyed the peace and quiet, and no one disturbed me as I rode along the narrow paths among the former factory buildings.

While I was riding, I noticed some teenagers standing in one of the corners. As I neared them they struck up a conversation with me, and I, in my innocence, did not identify the look of trouble in their eyes. One of them asked me for my bike. Naturally I refused to hand it over, and he tried to convince me that he only wanted to borrow it for a short ride around the factory. I continued to refuse, and he then started swearing at me and calling me names. I took the risk of hurling back a retort or two (you see, I wasn't all *that* shy!), and they acted as if they were offended. They used this as an excuse to start beating me up.

They really gave me a beating — I didn't know people could be so cruel. The one who had started up with me was the worst. It was as if he unleashed on me a terrible violence that was pent up. I was no match for him, and before I knew it he had knocked me down. That did not stop him from giving me more forceful blows and kicks, and his friends helped. I cried and begged them to stop, but they ignored my pleas. Then everything turned black and I fainted.

When I came to, they had disappeared — along with my bike. Somehow I dragged myself to the street, where someone caught sight of me and took me home. My parents took me to the hospital, where I was found to have internal bleeding, fractures, and other injuries. The doctor in the emergency room described my attackers as beasts, not human beings. My physical injuries eventually healed, but the mental damage was far greater.

I was a sensitive boy, who was not even accustomed to shouts, not to mention physical force, at home. These boys in their attack had humiliated my very being. It was not just the physical blows. What really hurt was that they treated me as if I were a worthless object. They beat me mercilessly and left me lying there like a piece of garbage. Then they ran off with my bike! They did not care at all about what would happen to me.

I felt as if they had murdered me. They had left me physically alive but inside I felt dead.

The factory has since been torn down and several new

buildings now stand in its place. Yet to this day whenever I pass the site I think to myself, "I was murdered on this spot." When I see children playing there, I want to tell them they are playing on my grave. This may sound exaggerated to you, Rabbi Walder, but such was the extent of the emotional damage I suffered.

I never shared my pain with anyone, and my parents never knew that I carried it inside. Once, I tried to tell a fellow *bachur* at yeshivah but he did not seem to want to hear. I think he just didn't know what to say, so he changed the subject. I decided then that I would never discuss the matter again with anyone — it would remain my own painful secret and I would get on with rebuilding my life.

From the outside, I succeeded — I got accepted into a good yeshivah and was a serious student. Although I still had occasional painful flashbacks about the attack, I somehow managed to live with it.

Rabbi Walder, I have told you Chapter One of my story, which takes us to the present. Chapter Two follows next.

My sister became engaged a few weeks ago. I knew she was going out with someone and I prayed with all my heart that things would work out for her because she had already been out on a lot of *shidduchim*. When I received my mother's message to come home from yeshivah for the celebration, I was overjoyed. At long last the *simchah* we were waiting for!

When the day came, I helped with the preparations and waited impatiently to meet the *chasan*. Our friends and relatives arrived and the house was filled with joy and excitement. Then there was a knock on the door, and my mother announced: "Here comes the *chasan*!" She opened the door, and standing in the doorway was ... it's almost too painful for me to write...

I came face to face with my attacker, my murderer — that's

how I thought of him.

Although six years had passed, I recognized him at once, and I was sure that he would identify me. But he didn't.

I was terrified. I had imagined that face in every dark alley and street for six years. It had haunted me. It was the face of the devil. Now here he was in my house, smiling, about to become my brother-in-law. He shook my hand as if we were meeting for the first time.

Throughout the evening, I tried to make sure not to be in the same room with him. I was shaking all over and my mother just couldn't understand why. She explained to everyone that it was due to over-excitement.

I didn't know what to do. On the one hand, I wanted to stand up and tell everyone who the *chasan* really was, and break up the *shidduch*. However, I was frightened and ashamed.

I did nothing.

The wedding is set for a month from today. My sister is going to marry an evil person. Will it ruin her life? Should I stop the wedding? Or will *that* ruin her life? Rabbi Walder, you are the only person I can turn to. Please read out my story on your program and tell me what to do.

Author's note:

As a result of this letter, the writer was contacted. The question of the *chasan* was examined and clarified by trustworthy people, and it turned out that the *chasan* had indeed gone through a period of crisis and great difficulty in his youth. However, he had received help and today was praised as a young man with a sensitive, excellent character.

The genuine regret he expressed, and his heartfelt apology to his former victim, turned out to be the most effective treatment for the emotional recovery of the injured youth.

That Disease

D ear Rabbi Walder,

I am an avid listener to your program and I know that lots of the stories you read out are short and to the point, have a surprise ending, and are sad — well, my story fits all those categories perfectly.

I am a 15-year-old high-school girl. Since seventh grade, I have had one really close friend — Michal. We are inseparable, and I think our kind of friendship is rare. We are always in and out of each other's houses, and we feel completely at home with each other's families.

Some time ago, my friend Michal began complaining that she wasn't feeling well. Her doctor said it was a virus, and assured her that it would pass. But it didn't, and he sent her for various tests. The results came back. To make a long story short, Michal was diagnosed as having what my parents call "that disease" — the one whose name people are afraid to say. The disease was found in her lungs, which is a particularly difficult type to cure.

Michal and I were devastated. We spoke for hours and I tried to raise her spirits and encourage her, but she was very depressed. She was sure she didn't have a chance of surviving, of recovering. As if that weren't enough, my mother didn't want me to visit Michal in the hospital! She kept giving me various jobs to do whenever I had free time, and I gradually came to realize that she asked me to do these tasks just when I was planning to go and visit Michal.

When I asked her if she was trying to keep me from visiting my best friend, she answered, in a hushed voice, that I was right — she was making it difficult for me to visit Michal. She did not want me to see her anymore.

I was at a loss to understand my mother's attitude. As I sat there crying and arguing, my father tried to calm me down, explaining that my mother was terrified of "that disease" because her father had passed away from it, and she wanted to keep me far away from anything or anyone connected with it. Also, my mother added, she had heard that a famous Chasidic rebbe used to say that if you don't mention "that disease" by its real name, then you won't get it.

"Okay, I won't mention the name," I tried to pacify my mother.

"Just being in contact with someone who suffers from 'that disease' might harm you!"

"But you know it isn't contagious!"

"I know, darling, but nevertheless I don't want you have the slightest contact with 'that disease'."

My mother's opposition was so strong that I had no choice but to give in. This upset Michal, who sent me a message asking me why I didn't come. I replied that I was sick, and the doctors said I couldn't visit anyone in the hospital for fear of infecting the other patients. However, I later found out that someone had let Michal know that I was perfectly healthy. Michal figured that I didn't want to see her, and so she stopped sending me messages.

Her mother then called my mother to try and find out why I

had abandoned my best friend when she needed me so badly. My mother tried to evade giving a direct answer, but finally she admitted that she was the one who would not allow me to visit Michal and she also explained her reasoning.

Michal's mother was shocked and hurt, and slammed the phone down on my mother. Of course my mother was quite upset over this, but she remained adamant: "I am quite prepared for the whole world to be angry with me if it is for the sake of my daughter's well-being."

I sent letters to Michal, telling her how much I missed her, and how I would love to visit her. Then one day Michal sent me a letter with another friend begging me to stop sending her letters, because they made her miss me so much. She added that she was not angry with me, because she knew why I wasn't visiting her. She told me that whenever she thought of me, it broke her heart and made her feel even sicker.

I turned to Hashem and prayed to Him to put other thoughts in my mother's mind so that she would let me visit Michal. I cannot tell you how many *tefillos* I prayed and how many tears I cried, begging Hashem to let me see her again.

Hashem answered my prayers.

One day shortly afterwards I got a severe headache. My mother took me to the doctor, who prescribed medication. The pills did not ease the pain, so we went back to the doctor, who said not to worry. Rabbi Walder, this sounds awfully familiar, doesn't it! Well, to make a long story short, I underwent a whole battery of tests and the end result was, yes — can you believe it? I have "that disease" in my brain.

My prayers were answered, but what will become of me?

Michal and I are in the same ward in the hospital, together — just as I prayed for.

Rabbi Walder, when you read out this story, I am sure there will be listeners who will know who we are, because our case is quite well-known.

Michal and I have a black sense of humor and joke a lot about things that aren't at all funny, like the fact that we're both bald because of the treatments we are having. We are convinced of one thing — that nothing will come between us anymore. Please ask your listeners to pray that we have a complete recovery and stay together in life, Amen.

The Teacher

Dear Rabbi Walder,

I have been a teacher for many years. The first four years of my career were one long nightmare. I am not exaggerating when I say I cannot recall a single good day during those years. My pupils didn't listen to me, and I couldn't control the class. They didn't learn anything, and spent most of their energy finding ways to make trouble for me. I taught at four different schools — one year at each school. Towards the end of each school year, I received the dreaded summons to the Principal's office. I knew exactly what he would say: "I know you try very hard, Yaakov, but things are not working out well..."

I had begun my teaching career eagerly, full of good intentions and great hopes. The entire first year was too terrible for words. I tried to be a friend to my pupils, I would tell them stories, I would reward them with prizes. Nothing succeeded. Chaos reigned in the classroom. By the time I decided to be stricter, it was too late — they knew I was only putting on an act, and they paid no attention to me. Every night I lay awake dreading what was awaiting me in the morning.

The second year, I decided to be strict with my pupils from the beginning — but then the parents complained to the Principal, who told me to be more gentle. My pupils quickly caught on to the fact that I had been reprimanded, and they proceeded to make my life miserable, knowing there was not a lot I could do. Looking back, I think the second year was even worse than the first.

The third year, I tried to find the correct balance between being strict and gentle, but my pupils were — this may sound extreme, but this is what I felt — merciless. They simply ruined my life. I began to hate my work. My self-esteem was shattered. Occasionally I would plead with them, "Stop it! What have I done to you to deserve this?" But they would laugh in my face.

Things reached a breaking point towards the end of the fourth year. When I was informed that I would not be teaching there the following year, my students heard about it and their misbehavior reached new heights. When I realized that I saw them as my enemies, I decided I was no longer fit to be a member of the teaching profession.

I went to speak to my Rebbe, Rav Fried, at the yeshivah where I had earned my teaching certificate in a special teaching program for yeshivah students. When I began to tell him of my teaching troubles, I broke down and cried like a small child. I was full of shame that I, who had been considered such a Torah scholar and a promising teacher, couldn't control a classroom of ten-year-olds. Rabbi Fried listened patiently, and then he gave me words of encouragement and *chizuk* to raise my spirits. He also provided me with some practical advice: "Think back to your own schooldays, Yaakov," he said, smiling. "Did you ever treat a teacher badly?"

In a flash I remembered Mr. Roseman! I was flooded with memories of how we had terrorized him! How we had mimicked his accent! How we had laughed at him! When he got angry and shouted at us, we would continue laughing. The truth is that he was a wonderful man, but was just too old and too impatient for a bunch of unruly schoolboys like us. He never tired of telling us how he had taught generations of pupils, and how none of them had caused him as much trouble as we did.

Perhaps Hashem was punishing me, measure for measure (*middah k'neged middah*)?

I decided then and there that I would try to find Mr. Roseman, go to him and beg his forgiveness.

Within three days I was standing at his door. His wife greeted me politely and showed me into the room where he was sitting. Entering the room, I hardly recognized the frail, elderly gentleman who greeted me politely. I introduced myself and asked him if he remembered me. No, he said, he didn't. I knew that if I mentioned one of my more infamous pranks, he would immediately remember me, but I chose not to remind him. Instead I told him that I was now a teacher, and was having a very difficult time with my pupils — to the extent that I was contemplating leaving the teaching profession.

Nodding sadly, he described to me his final years as a teacher, and how he was forced to resign when he suffered a stroke, probably brought on by his frustration and anger at his wayward pupils. "Oh, those boys," he sighed. "On the one hand they brought meaning to my life, but on the other..."

I took a deep breath and plucked up every ounce of courage I possessed: "Mr. Roseman, I think I am one of those pupils who...who may have brought on your suffering, and I have come to apologize and beg your forgiveness."

My old teacher was visibly moved. Suddenly he remembered me and my classmates (perhaps he had recognized me before, but didn't let on). He listened quietly as I told him sorrowfully that I believed my failure as a teacher was a punishment to me for my terrible behavior towards him during my own schooldays.

Mr. Roseman began to cry. "I forgive you," he said in a

whisper. I sat wordlessly as his tears flowed, and finally he found his voice. "Don't think I am crying about your past behavior. No, my dear pupil, it's just that sitting with you now brings my own sorrows up. My only son lives abroad. He is married to a non-Jewish woman and has severed all connections with *Yiddishkeit*, and with his aging parents. So you see, not only did I fail to teach my pupils — but I failed miserably with my only son. Perhaps if I had done things differently, things would have turned out better... But now it's too late for 'if only.' I am approaching the end of my life."

I asked Mr. Roseman if I could do anything to atone for my past misdeeds to him.

"I am a sick, old man, virtually on my deathbed, Yaakov. I will tell you — it causes me great pain to think that there will be almost no one attending my funeral. No son, no grandchildren. If you sincerely want to do something for me, then I would ask this: Please contact my former pupils and request that they be present at my funeral. I believe that some of them may even have liked me... and others may feel remorse for their behavior, as you do."

I told Mr. Roseman that it seemed somewhat awkward to organize attendance at a funeral of a person who was still alive, and wished him long life, "*ad me'ah v'esrim* — until 120!"

"Yes, yes," he said, "but you can just call them and tell them to be on standby. I suggest you organize a few of your former classmates and put each person in charge of calling an entire grade, so that perhaps even hundreds of my pupils will come to bid me a final farewell." His voice sounded strong, and his eyes seemed brighter. I told him I would do what I could.

This project appealed to me, and I decided that I would try to give Mr. Roseman the farewell party of his life as he departed for the World to Come. I contacted some of my former classmates, and we set things in motion. Within a short time I had organized a group of 25 friends, each of whom was responsible for contacting one class. All of his former pupils remembered Mr. Roseman, and many of them indeed felt guilty about their behavior towards him. They all readily agreed to attend his funeral when the time arrived, and all wished him long life as well.

I made a point of visiting Mr. Roseman now and again, and I told him of all those I had contacted. I also told him that they had all agreed to come to his funeral but in the meantime they were all concerned for his welfare and wished him many long years in this world. This moved him greatly, and he even laughed at the strange situation. Gradually we became close friends.

One day Mrs. Roseman called me to say that her husband was in the hospital. His condition had deteriorated dangerously. I rushed to see him and found him frailer and weaker than ever. With great difficulty, he managed to speak. "I really appreciate what you are doing for me, Yaakov. I forgive you completely, my dear pupil. May you be a successful teacher — unlike me."

These were his final words to me.

Within a few hours, thousands of his former pupils knew the time and place of the funeral.

It had been years since the cemetery in Haifa had seen such a large crowd attending a funeral. The vast majority of Mr. Roseman's former pupils showed up, and it was a strange combination of funeral and school reunion as people tried to identify their former classmates. Mr. Roseman's neighbors were very surprised to see thousands of people at the funeral of the quiet, modest schoolteacher.

I gave one of the eulogies and became very emotional. I spoke of Mr. Roseman. I spoke of how time flies by and we are able to achieve so little in life. I spoke about how we have to utilize our precious time in this world, and how we should rectify wrongs when we are able to. The school-reunion atmosphere slowly became a somber one as everyone mourned the loss of Mr. Roseman. I cried and the crowd cried with me. I wept for Mr. Roseman, for myself, for the past, and for the future. The funeral ended with all the former pupils saying *Kaddish* in unison for Mr. Roseman. A thousand *Kaddishes* instead of one absent son.

Rabbi Walder, that is the story of Mr. Roseman, and it is my story as well. More than I did for Mr. Roseman, I did for myself. I don't know how it happened, but after this episode I was no longer the same beleaguered person.

I left the elementary school and that fall I took up a new position in a high school, where I have had a successful teaching career for the sixteen years that have passed since then. I will never know if it was simply a case of "changing my place and changing my luck," or if it was due to the blessing of Mr. Roseman's final words to me.

Once a year, on Mr. Roseman's *yahrtzeit*, the entire student body of my school gathers together to hear my story and then I say *Kaddish*. This year, his *yahrtzeit* falls on a Sunday, the day of your program. I would be very pleased, Rabbi Walder, if you could read out my story and ask your listeners to pray for the *illui neshamah* of Mr. Roseman — *Moshe ben Yosef Chaim z"l.*

A "Friend" in Need

Dear Rabbi Walder,

I think my story contains an important lesson for people who may have encountered situations similar to mine.

In yeshivah, I was never really considered a serious student. I wasn't the kind that hung out on the streets, but still I didn't actually learn much either. You could say I just hung around within the building!

It wasn't always like that, though. When I was bar mitzvah age I was at the top of my class and I had no difficulty getting accepted into one of the best yeshivos. However, I was unaccustomed to the absence of strict supervision in my new yeshivah. No one checked attendance and I guess I was drunk with freedom. Within a short time I had lost my good study habits, and no one seemed to notice.

Around that time, I became friends with Danny. My parents did not approve of our friendship, but I didn't want to hear about their opposition. For lonely teenagers, friends can become the most important thing in life, even more important than the mitzvah of honoring one's parents — or even, God forbid, keeping mitzvos at all.

Until I met Danny, my soul was pure and innocent, even when I had stopped being a good student. There was never any doubt in my mind about my way of life. Then I saw how Danny made fun of praying, how he mocked our fellow students, and how he despised our religious way of life in general. At first I was genuinely shocked and upset and I tried to argue with him, but gradually I found myself joining in his mocking and slowly but surely my own fear of Heaven weakened and I also began to make fun of the religious life. Although I still dressed like a regular *yeshivah bachur*, inside I really was not religious. So many Rebbeim and good souls tried to convince me to break up my friendship with Danny, but nothing could tear me away from him. I was willing to do anything to keep his friendship — I was prepared to leave family, friends, yeshivah, and — I admit — even *Yiddishkeit*, in order to remain close to Danny.

When we were together I felt smart, happy and full of confidence. When we started to hang around on the streets, we needed money for food and clothes. Danny and I found "ways and means" of getting hold of cash. We were very creative, and we would use every word except the accurate term — stealing — to describe our activities. We quickly spiraled down into the murky world of crime. The lowest point was when we were involved in a particularly serious crime — but I do not wish to elaborate.

I was like someone who had reached the bottom of a pit. There was only one direction for me — upwards. I missed Torah study and I found myself beginning to long for the *beis midrash*. Slowly, slowly, I tried to climb up and mend my ways, but Danny did everything in his power to drag me back down. He begged me not to abandon him. I promised that I would never leave him, but that I just wanted to spend some time in the *beis midrash*. He realized, though, that if I got back again onto the right path, I would inevitably leave him. And that was too much for him to bear.

One day, Danny threatened me that if I didn't accompany him to a certain place, he would inform my parents of the "story." He didn't have to elaborate — we both knew he was referring to that terrible crime.

By now I had discovered something about my "friend" — that he was no friend, he never was my friend, and never would be. He was not interested in my welfare at all; he thought only of himself. I faced Danny squarely and informed him of this truth. A bitter and acrimonious argument followed and at the end of it we had become firm enemies. At least he no longer wanted to hang out with me — after all, who wants to have fun with an enemy!

But if I thought I had heard the last of Danny, I was mistaken. One day he called me to inform me that I owed him money.

"For what?" I asked.

"I've made an account of how much money I spent on you, and now I want it back!"

"Danny, are you crazy? The money was never yours in the first place — you know very well where it came from."

"Listen, I don't care where the money came from. All I know is that you used more than I did and now I want it back. You're glad to be back in yeshivah? If you don't pay, be sure that the Rosh Yeshivah will receive certain information from me about your past. You won't last another day there."

I succumbed to the threat and borrowed money to pay Danny. This did not turn out to be a one-time payment, and his demands only grew. He was constantly blackmailing me with the threat that if I didn't pay up, he would go to the Rosh Yeshivah with the story. I was anyhow haunted by my past and did not want it to compromise my future. This pattern continued for a few years. However, there was a red line Danny knew I would never cross. I would never again commit a crime. Once he even showed me a stamped envelope addressed to my Rosh Yeshivah. He threatened to mail it if I didn't agree to do what he was demanding at the time.

"Go ahead," I told him, "mail the letter. But I will never again break the law for you. I don't want you to have another reason to blackmail me."

Danny relented, and I wondered why I hadn't acted so firmly when he demanded cash. Some time later I heard through the grapevine that he was married. I sighed with relief, and I didn't hear from him for a long time.

I settled down well to yeshivah life, delved into learning, and worked on improving myself. I was considered a good *bachur*, but I knew that it was only a percentage of what I had been before I met Danny.

I still harbored a dark secret, and this frightened me when I started getting suggestions for *shidduchim*. I decided to look for a down-to-earth, kind-hearted and forgiving girl who would allow me to unburden my secret so I would not have to spend my entire life living in fear.

When I met Batsheva, I realized she was the answer to my prayers. She was a kind, sympathetic, straightforward, and honest girl from a solid family. I would have preferred our engagement not be announced in the local newspaper, but I agreed to it. Who could have understood my fears? I prayed that Danny would not see the announcement.

I guess I didn't deserve that, and two days later, my former "friend" called and asked to meet with me. I was able to push him off for another two weeks. In the meantime, as I grew closer to Batsheva, I hoped she would believe in me as I was today.

Then I met with Danny, and he thrust a letter at me. "This letter contains all the sordid details about your past and your part in that crime. I know that your bride comes from a wealthy family, and I am sure you don't want her to know the truth about you. For the sum of $10,000, I am prepared to forget everything and leave you alone to build your future. However, if you do not agree to pay, this letter will be sent to Batsheva."

There was no point in arguing with Danny. I knew I was dealing with a ruthless criminal who would have no hesitation about ruining my life.

"Danny, give me two weeks to raise the money."

"No problem. I know you're marrying a rich girl and the wedding is set for six weeks from now. I have patience."

I went straight from the meeting with Danny to ask a leading Rabbi in Bnei Brak for his advice. Once I was admitted to his room, I closed the door and told him the whole story, crying as I unburdened myself. The Rabbi was very kind and patient. He asked me about my relationship with Batsheva, and he advised me how to make the bond between us even stronger and at the same time how to prepare her for the blow she was about to receive from Danny. He said that from his experience, a blackmailer cannot change himself and that Danny would find a way sooner or later to reveal the truth about my past to Batsheva. He said that from my description, Danny was a heartless, cruel person in addition to being a blackmailer and would send the letter whether I paid him or not. The Rav told me to play for time as long as possible, and then to inform the police. As I left, he told me that only with many prayers would I succeed. He spelled out certain mitzvos that I should take on, to earn Hashem's forgiveness (*baruch Hashem*, my sin was one that I could repent for).

I followed the Rav's instructions and played for time for two weeks. During that time, I was busy praying and putting all my heart into my Torah study. In the evenings, I would spend time with Batsheva, developing the trust and closeness between us. When I hinted to her that I had gone through a rough time in the past, she was very understanding and said that the only thing that mattered to her was what I am now, because everyone can slip. I thought to myself that not everyone errs as much as I did, but I didn't dare say it.

Two weeks later, I called Danny to tell him that a savings plan of mine was due to mature in another ten days so he would have to wait. Danny sounded impatient and threatened me that if I didn't give him the entire amount in cash in ten days, he would send the letter immediately. What Danny didn't know was that I had taped the conversation.

A week later I reported the matter to the police. Blackmail is considered a serious crime, and they took down all the details of my complaint. I was very grateful that they were not interested in the crime Danny was threatening to reveal. The police told me to set up a meeting with Danny at an arranged time and place, and they would send plain-clothes policeman there. They would first attach a recording device to me. They instructed me how to speak to Danny so that they would be able to charge him with blackmail and threatening behavior. The police assured me they would do their utmost to ensure that the letter would not reach Batsheva, although, they told me, in their experience a blackmailer usually carries out his threat even though he has been warned that it will only make matters worse for him. They explained that Danny probably would not give up until Batsheva received the letter.

I arranged to meet Danny the following Wednesday at a certain restaurant. When he arrived, I tried to persuade him to stop blackmailing me. He was very harsh and threatened me over and over again. He did not mince his words and threatened that if I did not pay up he would not only send the letter to Batsheva, but he would also see to it that I would be in physical danger. Finally, we agreed to meet the following day at the same place, and I promised to bring the cash with me. As soon as Danny was out of sight, I handed the recording of our conversation to the police, and they said they would also be at the meeting the following day.

When Danny turned up, I handed him an envelope containing the cash, and he handed me the letter. Before he had a chance to open the envelope, three policemen put him under arrest.

All this took place about two weeks before my wedding, and now I was in a race against time. If Danny was released from jail before my wedding, I knew the letter would be mailed. I had to summon all my emotional energy to testify at the police station and then come home and pretend that everything was just fine. Even under the best of circumstances, the days preceding a wedding can be tense and hectic, so my family just figured I had pre-wedding nerves.

The police detained Danny for fourteen days, meaning that he would be released three days before the wedding. I explained my situation to an understanding officer, and he promised he would warn Danny not to send the letter to Batsheva. I know that a marriage should be based on honesty, but I was just too frightened to acknowledge that trying to keep this from her wasn't really the right thing to do.

I spent the three days prior to my wedding in a state of extreme anxiety. I considered this to be part of my sincere repentance for my past misdeeds. I was physically nauseous with fear. Our custom was that the bride and groom not meet for the week before the wedding, so I phoned Batsheva every day, fearing the worst. I was still terrified that the letter from Danny would arrive before our wedding.

The great day finally came, and there was no sign of the letter. I stood under the *chuppah* crying and praying to Hashem that we merit His blessing in setting up a true Jewish home. During the dinner I danced with great joy, thanking Hashem for my happiness. I also felt a tremendous release of tension for all I had been through these past few months. Danny's letter no longer frightened me, for I knew that nothing could ever come between Batsheva and me.

One day, during the week of *sheva berachos*, when we visited Batsheva's parents, her mother handed us a letter that had come — *the* letter. I casually took it from her, telling Batsheva that I'd put it safely in my pocket and she could open it at home.

In the safety of our own home, I poured out my heart to Batsheva, telling her about my "friend" Danny who wants to tell her about my past so that he can break up our marriage. She told me she wasn't interested in the slightest in reading such a letter. To my immense relief, she told me that she was happy with me as I was now and that nothing else interested her. I thanked Hashem for sending me such a wonderful wife.

The following day, I handed Danny's letter to the police, who transferred it to the judge in charge of the case. He ordered Danny to be remanded in custody until the end of the proceedings.

Danny was sentenced to community service and given a two-year suspended sentence. However, his real punishment was the breakup of his marriage. When his wife heard about his misdeeds, she demanded a divorce.

Rabbi Walder, I am sending you this story on my first wedding anniversary. Batsheva now knows everything about me, and *baruch Hashem* that it didn't cause any friction between us. She knows that I have done a complete and sincere *teshuvah*.

We decided to send you our story in the hope that your many teenage listeners will hear it read on your program. I hope that it will teach them to take a good look at their friends. The adolescent years can be lonely ones, and it is so easy to fall prey to a "friend" who seems to offer warmth and love, but in reality is only out for his own good and can ruin your future. I would tell young people: Listen to your parents and your teachers — they truly love you and care about you.

The other important lesson I have learned is never, ever to give in to blackmail. The Rav in Bnei Brak told me, "Once a blackmailer, always a blackmailer." It's better to pay a heavy price once than continually be under the threat of blackmail. Unfortunately, this phenomenon is not uncommon. There are a lot of youngsters with a secret to hide and evil people who resort to blackmail, threatening to reveal their secret and thus give them and their families a bad reputation and harm their chances for a good *shidduch*. I can only beg these young people not to succumb, but to tell their parents or a Rav who is not personally involved. Rabbi Walder, I think that this program and your *KidSpeak* series are an excellent address.

One winter evening, Batsheva and I were sitting at home enjoying a quiet moment together. I felt so safe and secure and remarked to my wife that it was very cold outside. She knew from my tone that I wasn't referring to the weather, but to the emotional and spiritual cold of the loneliness experienced by so many youngsters. I searched for warmth and thought I had found it in Danny, but I learned the hard way that he had nothing to offer me. I discovered true love and warmth in my parents' home and in a true Jewish life — which I am privileged to share with my *eishes chayil* Batsheva.

Fathers and Sons

Dear Rabbi Walder,

My name is Zacharya. I am a man in my sixties, and most of my nine children are married already. I live on a *moshav* and have a small farm. I am not as young or strong as I used to be, but when I was younger, I was a very tough person. I worked hard and demanded a lot from myself and from others.

My children's upbringing was the most important thing in my life. I had lots of principles, and I was very strict. Looking back, I can see now that I was probably too harsh. I probably got angry too easily. My children were afraid of me and never dared to do anything stupid for fear of my temper! On the other hand, they knew that all of my hard work was for them. I was happy to live with just the basic necessities as long as their futures were provided for. Over and over again I told my children how I didn't care at all about my own personal comfort. All I cared about was raising them to become decent, God-fearing, hard-working adults.

I admit that it wasn't easy. Sometimes, the children would rebel against my demands. Looking back, I can remember great tension at home during such periods. I would yell and threaten, promise them presents if they behaved and punish them when they didn't. I cared about everything they did — and I was forever pointing out to them that in return, I did not expect to have disobedient children. Those years can be characterized by the expression *tza'ar gidul banim*, "the pain of raising children."

My next-door neighbor, Rafi D., was the exact opposite of me. He was a calm, relaxed father. I never once heard him even raise his voice to his children. He simply let them do whatever they wanted! And he didn't save and scrimp like I did. Their house was furnished beautifully, and they always had a new car. My wife often complained to me, "Zecharya, you earn as much as Rafi does, and you never think of buying new furniture. Every penny has to go into savings. Take an example from Rafi — he thinks about himself too, and his children are good kids."

Rabbi Walder, I must admit that her complaints really hurt me. I sometimes wondered if I was simply stupid for working so hard for my children and fighting with them so much, when they just caused me trouble. Sometimes I took it out on them too: "Why am I working so hard for you children? Just to see how badly you behave towards me?"

My neighbor on the other side once tried to tell me that I was not educating my children properly, that I expected too much from them and I was too harsh. However, I believed in my ways and couldn't imagine how a person who cared about his children could not want to have strict control over them.

The years passed, the boys went off to learn in yeshivos, my children grew up, and one by one they all got married. And then — an amazing thing happened. As they each set up their own homes, they began to go out of their way to honor me. Each one would call me every day to see how my wife and I were. They came over for visits whenever they could. They constantly offered to help us. I was astonished at the transformation. They had always been solicitous of their mother, but I could not fathom how they suddenly became so concerned about their father!

My neighbor Rafi also married off his children, but in his case it was no easy task because he had not put away savings for them over the years, and he refused to take out loans to help them get married. His children left the area one by one when they got married.

Over the next few years we were blessed with grandchildren. We made it a rule that each daughter or daughter-in-law who gave birth would come straight from the hospital to our house for ten days of "five-star hotel" treatment. I continued to work as hard as usual, and my savings were now put away for our grandchildren.

My neighbor Rafi and his wife did not see their grandchildren very often. Their children would only come for the holidays, and then Mrs. D. would complain to my wife how hard it was for them to host their children and grandchildren, and how they would heave a sigh of relief when they left. She added that Rafi couldn't stand the noise and the mess.

One day, out of the blue, I got sick. It turned out that I had a serious kidney disease, and my health deteriorated rapidly. Before long, I was undergoing dialysis every day. I was always accompanied by one of my sons. This went on for three years, and I began to wish I would die rather than live like that. The doctor discussed with me the idea of having a kidney transplant.

"Unfortunately, Zacharya," he said, "there is a waiting list, and it could take years, unless you can find a relative with a suitable kidney."

My son Yaakov was there that day. "Doctor, I'll be happy to be a donor," he said immediately.

"What?" I said. "I will not let any of my children endanger

their lives for me. You need your own kidneys!"

A few days later, when several of my sons happened to be visiting, I was resting in my room, and I fell asleep. Suddenly I was awakened by shouts coming from the kitchen. At first I was confused by all the noise, but gradually I recognized my sons' voices — I hadn't heard raised voices in our house for a long time — and I realized that they were in the midst of a fierce argument. And about what? About who would have the privilege of donating a kidney to me! Eliezer, my oldest son, said it was *his* right as the firstborn. Binyamin, my youngest, claimed that he had received the most from me, so he wanted to be the donor. Yaakov insisted that since he had been with me at the hospital and had immediately volunteered, then he should be allowed to fulfill his commitment.

In tears, I went down to the kitchen and hugged and kissed each one of my sons. "My dear children," I told them, crying like a child, "I don't deserve your devotion to me. I should be begging your forgiveness for all the times I was so harsh with you." Tears of regret for all my past wrongdoings flowed freely.

My sons calmed me down, and told me that they remembered only my devotion to them, and how I lived only for them and not for myself. One of my sons went so far as to say that he would be prepared to donate his heart to me, and his words made everyone in the room cry.

In the end, my children went to a Rabbinical court to settle the "dispute." This case received a fair amount of local coverage, and it's possible that you, Rabbi Walder, even heard about it. The *dayanim* decided that Eliezer, my oldest son, would have the privilege of donating his kidney — not just because of his status as the firstborn but also because it turned out that he was the most suitable match.

The transplant was successful.

Afterwards, I essentially retired, and began to discover the pleasures of being at home. My neighbor Rafi and I spent a lot of time chatting together, and he was forever complaining about his children. They hardly visited and didn't seem to care about their parents much. I was at a loss to answer him.

Fall arrived and with it the wonderful Festival of Sukkos. Naturally, my children all came over right after Yom Kippur, and within a short time they had erected a huge *sukkah* in the garden. They wouldn't let me do a thing, just the symbolic act of putting some *sechach* on the roof so that I would merit the mitzvah of erecting the *sukkah*.

The next day, I noticed my neighbor Rafi go into his garden shed and, with great physical effort, take out planks of wood and set about building his *sukkah*. After a short time, he just sat down, holding his head in despair.

I went over to him. "Rafi, what's the matter? Is it too hard for you?"

"Zecharya," he said in a broken voice, "I called each one of my children and asked them if they could spare a couple of hours to help me put up the *sukkah*. But they were all too busy, and gave me some reason why they couldn't come."

I listened to Rafi with tears in my eyes. This was my always placid neighbor who was now pouring out his heart to me.

"I just don't understand it," he went on. "I never punished them, never yelled at them, and now? Now they just ignore me. I gave them an easy, happy childhood — why don't they want to pay me back?"

I said nothing in reply, even though I had some idea of how to answer him. When I went home I immediately picked up the phone and called Aharon, Rafi's oldest son. Aharon lived in a town some distance away, and I knew that he was having trouble earning a living because he had recently asked me if I could help him find an extra job.

"Hello, Aharon, this is Zecharya speaking. How would you like to earn $100 for two hours of work?"

"That's a lot of money," he said. "What's the work?"

"Oh, there's an old man I know who has no one to help him build his *sukkah*. I also have someone who wants to give $100 to whoever agrees to do it. I know that I can find somebody around here easily, but I thought of you first because you told me you're looking for extra work."

Aharon immediately agreed to my offer and said he would take the first bus. We fixed a time to meet at the bus station and from there, I told him, we would take a cab to the old man's house.

Everything went according to plan, and once settled in the taxi, I turned to him and said, "Aharon, I am the one who's paying the $100, and your father is the old man who needs help with his *sukkah*." I looked him straight in the eyes. At first he looked angry, but his anger quickly turned to shame. He looked away, and tried to make all kinds of excuses about how he had been busy when his father had called him for help.

"Listen, Aharon," I said, "our two families grew up next door to each other. I was a strict, tyrannical father. I demanded a lot from my children, and maybe I went too far sometimes. I expected them to learn from me, even to think as I did. Yet now, they love me and honor me, take care of my every need, build the *sukkah* for me, do all the shopping before Pesach, and make sure that my wife and I are never alone for Shabbos.

"I wonder if you heard about the *din Torah* that had to decide which child would donate a kidney to me, because each of my children fought for the right to be the donor! I was embarrassed.

"But you, Aharon, you were a child who had a peaceful, happy childhood. Your father never shouted at you or criticized you or demanded anything of you. He never punished you. And this is how you show your gratitude? Your father is a good man and his children have shown no thanks to him for their wonderful upbringing. Don't you know that one of the Ten Commandments is 'Honor your father and your mother'?"

It took Aharon several minutes before he replied. "Zecharya, you are absolutely right about the mitzvah of honoring one's parents. I have nothing to say in my defense. However, regarding the rest of your comments I won't go into detail, but I'll just tell you a few things and you can draw your own conclusions."

He took a deep breath. "A father who doesn't ever get angry at his son or criticize him is not necessarily being kind to him. It's not so much because of an educational philosophy, but rather because of the absence of such a philosophy! It's not really love or pity that such a father is showing his son — it's indifference! Perhaps such a father cares more about his own well-being than his child's.

"King Solomon was thinking of such parents when he wrote in *Mishlei*, 'Spare the rod, hate the child.' These parents just want peace and quiet and can't be bothered arguing with their children. They don't want the trouble and conflict that come from saying no, or the confrontation that demands strength. Their personal comfort is more important to them than their child's upbringing. Do you think that children want to do exactly as they please, Zecharya? No, the opposite is true. Believe me, I've thought about this a lot. Children need boundaries, and strong parents who will keep them from doing wrong. They need and want guidance, parents who will tell them what to do and who will punish them if they fail to do it. Like you did. True, a child is obligated to respect his parents because it is a commandment in the Torah — but his heart may tell him otherwise.

"Zecharya, your children had a difficult father, it's true. But they knew their father *cared* about them. You took great interest in their upbringing, in all the details of their lives. You might have made mistakes, but your children knew that you were there for them, that you were more devoted to them than to yourself. They knew that you were strong, that you never lowered your expectations of them, and that you never demanded of them more than you demanded of yourself.

"I know that when we were younger, your children were jealous of us because we had such a peaceful home, where we were never asked to do anything, and we were never punished! But, believe me, as one grows older, one begins to see things from a different perspective. Your children grew to appreciate your devotion to them and now they cannot do enough to show you their love and gratitude, whereas we..." Aharon sighed.

The taxi pulled up to the house.

"Just go to your father now," I said, "and please don't tell him about this conversation. Tell him that you decided to surprise him and come and build the *sukkah* for him."

Aharon did as I requested, and I went to my own house and sat on my porch watching him work and reflecting on all the amazing things he had said.

Suddenly, I heard Rafi calling me. "Look, Zecharya! Aharon decided to surprise me, and he came to build my *sukkah*." He lowered his voice so his son wouldn't hear. "I guess my children do care about me after all."

"I told you so, Rafi. Look how hard Aharon is working — that's a devoted son you have."

But I thought to myself, "Devoted to his father or to $100?"

Time would tell. In the meantime I had a lot to think about.

A Barber's Tale

Dear Rabbi Walder,
        I may be one of your oldest listeners, and judging from the letters you read, I'm probably the oldest person to write to you. Actually, I wouldn't even know about your program if my children hadn't insisted that I listen every week.

My name is Solly and I am eighty years old. From the age of eighteen I have been a barber. I began my career as a barber's assistant in my village in Morocco and I quickly discovered that I had "golden hands" as a barber — I never had professional training, and I just had to look at a person to know instinctively what hairstyle would suit him.

After several years as an assistant, I left the village and opened my own shop in the city of Meknès. It was a successful venture, and before long all the fashionable young men in the town were coming to me because they knew that for me, haircutting was an art. I had no choice but to take on an assistant to take over some of the work. I chose my childhood friend Maurice, who had tried to open his own barbershop in the village, but had not been able to make a living.

Things didn't work out exactly as I had planned, unfortunately. My clients continued to wait in line specifically for me, while Maurice continued to wait for customers to come to him. He would sit in his chair looking expectantly at the customers, hoping that one of them would want him. The clients would avert their glances out of embarrassment.

We finally came to an arrangement that young children and elderly people who were only interested in a simple, standard haircut would go to Maurice, and the young men who wanted a stylish haircut would come to me.

In the 1950s I came to Israel with my whole family, and I set up a barbershop in Ramat Gan. My initial clients were former customers from Morocco, but my reputation spread by word of mouth and the business was flourishing within a short time. Eventually, members of Knesset and other notables joined my clientele, and I was well-known.

Maurice followed me faithfully, and the working arrangement that we'd had in Morocco continued in Israel. When there were no young children or elderly people who needed a simple haircut, Maurice would try to interest my clients in coming to him, but he always received the same answer from the embarrassed customers: "Sorry, but I prefer to wait in line for Solly."

As my sons grew up, they decided to join me in the shop and it soon became apparent that my hairdressing skills had passed on to the next generation. Each one became a talented barber, and one of them, Uri, graduated from a professional hairdressing school. When Uri set up his own barbershop, he called it a "salon." My other three sons followed in his footsteps — they spent a few years with me improving their skills and then moved on to open their own "salons."

Thus time passed. One year followed another, and I grew older. My clients also grew older, and the young men chose to go to younger barbers. In the good old days, I would have five to six clients an hour, then it dwindled to two or three, and then to an occasional customer. The rest of the time I would sit around, chatting with Maurice and waiting for business. Whenever I did get a customer, I made sure to take a long time cutting his hair — it made the day pass faster. Maurice's task was now reduced to sweeping the floor — and as each hair fell from a customer's head he would sweep it up. Thus he was always getting in my way, which began to annoy me.

It didn't take him long to come to the logical conclusion, and one day Maurice informed me that he had decided to retire.

I did not know how to react to Maurice's announcement, and so I sat silently watching him gather his few possessions. I could only nod silently when my assistant of over fifty years waved goodbye and walked out of the shop.

Working on my own turned out to be much harder than I thought. It took me time to realize that in fact I couldn't manage without Maurice. I had become so used to his presence that I now found myself longing for his idle chatter and even for the many arguments we'd had over the years. I suddenly felt very old, and life became a burden. Exactly one year after Maurice's retirement I came to the conclusion that it was time for me to follow suit, so I closed the shop and went home.

My son Uri saw that I was depressed, and he offered me a job in his salon. I agreed, and I looked forward enthusiastically to spending my time productively again. I suddenly felt years younger at the prospect of being busy. Uri's salon was very fancy, and he had a top-class reputation. How good it would be to lighten his workload.

On the first day, I arrived early at the salon — even before Uri. I hadn't been able to sleep the night before, from excitement. I first had a number of young children, and when I had finished with them I announced to the other people who were waiting for their turn that I was free. Several people continued staring past me into space as if they hadn't heard me, and the others buried their head in their newspaper. Not understanding, I asked again who was next for a haircut — but still no one made a move.

Then I understood.

I watched as Uri blushed and quietly went over to some of the people to convince them to come to me for their haircut. This was surely the most humiliating and degrading moment I have ever experienced in my life. I regretted the moment I had agreed to come and work for Uri. I wished the floor would open and swallow me up; that would have been better than the pitying looks on the faces of Uri's customers.

I think the worst of all was that I had been put to shame in front of my own son. And I knew exactly what he was feeling about my pathetic attempts to get customers — in a flash I had realized that Maurice must have felt like this all those years.

I walked out of Uri's salon silently and went home. I sat around feeling sorry for myself for some time, until I decided that I was not going to spend the last years of my life sitting at home and crying about my past glories. It was time to act. And I had an idea.

I dialed Maurice's number and asked him if I could come over for a visit. He sounded pleased to hear my voice and invited me over. We drank Turkish coffee and reminisced about the past. Then I told him what had happened to me in Uri's salon. Maurice listened silently. What could he say? He realized that I now knew how he had suffered for years in my salon.

Then I put forward my proposal: "Maurice, what would you think about us reopening the barbershop?"

"Well, Solly, that sounds like a good idea, but I'd still be hanging around doing nothing."

"So let's work in shifts. After all, the real reason for reopening the shop is so that we'll have something to do and people to talk to. If we work in shifts, I'm sure we'll both be satisfied."

We set about refurbishing the premises. We put new, modern ceramic tiles on the floor and walls, brought new comfortable chairs, and added lots of mirrors. The old barber shop now looked like a high-class salon. Rabbi Walder, many of your listeners are probably familiar with my shop. Then Maurice and I decided to do an experiment and employ a young hairdresser who would attract the younger clientele. We would concentrate on those who drop by, without an appointment, for a quick haircut — small children, old people, and Chasidim who just want their hair shaved and their *peyos* left alone and who couldn't care less about the age of the barber.

In the front window we put a large sign: "No appointment needed," and this brought in people who had no time to wait around.

Our idea paid off, and the salon attracted many new customers.

Rabbi Walder, I learned painfully that a person has to accept his age and not get depressed when he sees that younger people are taking over. This is the way of the world, and a person must be grateful for what there is. But from my own humiliation, I learned something else too. I learned how blind I had been to my friend's suffering for years, and *baruch Hashem*, there was still time to rectify the wrong.

Independence?

Dear Rabbi Walder,

Every week I listen to the readers' letters that you read on your program, and I often find myself crying in sympathy with their sad stories. In a way, though, I'm also crying for myself. You see, I too have a sad story, and in my case there is no happy ending. It is a story I live every hour of the day.

My husband and I are respected people in our community. We put all our efforts into giving our children a good education and for years we have worked hard and learned to forgo luxuries so that our children would not lack anything. Naomi, our eldest daughter, was always a pretty and charming girl. When she had difficulties in school, we hired the best private tutors; and if she had any social problems, we went all out to try and help her. Naomi was not a particularly diligent student, but she was proud and very independent.

The reason I stress this is that her independence mattered to her more than anything else. As soon as she entered her teenage years, she started to demonstrate her independence. Rabbi

Walder, don't misunderstand me; independence is a good trait, but my Naomi understood the concept as permission to be impudent and to refuse to accept even the slightest comment or rebuke from us. At the same time she felt she had a free hand to criticize us for everything we did or didn't do. An innocent comment on my part, like telling her that one of her buttons was hanging on its last thread, would get a response such as: "Mom, stop interfering. I can manage perfectly well by myself."

Now, I wasn't an interfering mother at all, Rabbi Walder. Quite the contrary — but Naomi's incessant need for independence was unconnected to anything I did or didn't do. Her teenage years were simply impossible. She talked back, criticized us about how we were raising our younger children, and insulted us — whereas it was unthinkable that *we* would comment on anything *she* did. At one point, when we'd had enough of her behavior and I decided it was time to put my foot down and be firm, and she went around telling her siblings and relatives what terrible parents we were. This only increased the growing distance between us.

When Naomi finished high school, my husband sent her to the expensive computer graphics courses she was interested in, and we bought her a top model computer. In her eyes, however, we remained the "wicked parents," and she the "unfortunate child."

Since Naomi was a pretty and outgoing girl, she was sought after by matchmakers. She told everyone that she couldn't wait to get married: "I want to get out of this house where people are always telling me what to do!"

When she was introduced to Motti, it didn't take more than a few dates until they decided to become engaged. The fact is, we were not enthusiastic about the match — there was something about him that made us nervous — but I think that was all the more reason for Naomi to *davka* choose him.

When the wedding day arrived, we put on a brave face and

acted happy. Inside, though, we were full of trepidation. After the wedding, Motti and Naomi moved to another city.

As the weeks went by, a pattern was established. The young couple never phoned us to say hello; it was always I who had to call them. I would visit them occasionally, and ask them to visit us, but Naomi was so excited by her new, independent status that she ignored my invitations.

When I realized she wasn't working, I asked her why. She had loved graphic design.

"Oh, Motti doesn't approve," she said breezily.

"What doesn't he approve of?"

"He doesn't want me going out to work."

"Well," I answered, taken aback, "I guess it's wonderful that he wants you to be a full-time housewife." I tried to sound enthusiastic, but her words tugged at my heart.

During the first two or three years, gradually all contact between us ceased. One day, Tova, her best friend from high school, gave me a call. She suggested gently that I check out what was going on in Naomi's house. Tova told me that she had gone to visit her, and Motti had told her to leave the house.

Realizing that all was not well with my daughter and her husband, at the first opportunity (the birth of their second daughter), I went to visit. In the course of our conversation, I mentioned Tova and asked Naomi if she knew how she was.

"Tova?" Motti interrupted. "I just threw her out of my house. I don't want her having any bad influence on my wife. I want Naomi to break all connections with people like that." I was so shocked I couldn't utter a word. Motti then went on to describe enthusiastically how he had humiliated Tova.

As soon as I could, I contacted all Naomi's close friends as well as her cousins to whom she was very attached. It turned out that they all had the same story to tell me: Naomi had terminated the friendship quickly and totally, and they were all taken by surprise. Moreover, they all assumed that Motti was the cause because he had always seemed to resent their calls, and made Naomi end the conversation.

As if all this were not bad enough, we were in for an even bigger shock. During one of their rare Shabbos visits to us, during the Friday night meal, the baby started crying and Naomi picked her up from the carriage and held her. Motti immediately ordered her to put the baby back; he didn't want the baby to "get spoiled," he stated. Naomi obediently put the baby back, but a few minutes later she began to cry again. Naomi instinctively picked her up, and — Boom!

Motti hit Naomi. The blow to her head was so strong that I was afraid he had fractured her skull. Naomi almost dropped the baby, and we rushed to take her. Naomi sat stunned for a few moments, and a terrible silence reigned in the room. There had never been any violence in our home. The situation seemed unreal, impossible. No one spoke. Naomi sighed. Motti got up and stalked out the house, presumably to go back to the neighbor's apartment where they were staying.

I brought Naomi a glass of cold water. No one knew what to do. *Baruch Hashem*, their older child was sleeping. My husband simply rushed through the rest of the meal and left the table. Our younger children retreated to their rooms.

I was left alone with Naomi.

"Naomi, my precious daughter, please, please let me help you," the words tumbled out. "You don't have to be the victim of such violence. Tell me, has he ever hit you before?" In my heart I knew that it wasn't the first time.

And what did my daughter say? "Mom, don't interfere! I want to be independent." Then she scooped up her daughters and walked out of the house. By her "cool" and unsurprised reaction, I realized that Naomi must suffer physical abuse from her husband regularly.

The next day was tense, but somehow we got through it. After that terrible Shabbos, Naomi severed all contact with us — I suppose Motti was ashamed to see us. We tried sending our rabbi, and others who could help, but Naomi was uncooperative.

Rabbi Walder, I wish I could end the story here, but it goes from bad to worse.

One day a relative called us and asked how Naomi was doing.

"Why do you ask?" I replied warily, sensing something in the tone of her voice.

"If I'm not mistaken," she said, and paused, "I think I saw her begging for money at the Tel Aviv Central Bus Station."

"What? Don't be silly! You must be mistaken."

It seemed so impossible that we didn't even bother to check out the matter.

To our dismay, however, the following week we received regards from Naomi from another relative who had seen her begging for money at a shopping mall, and acquaintances reported that she had knocked on their door as she went from house to house to beg for money. It was now clear that our "independent" daughter had become a beggar.

My husband and I made an appointment with a psychologist to try to understand the situation and see how we could help Naomi. The psychologist told us that Motti's behavior was typical of a certain personality disorder in which the husband severs all contact between his wife and her family and friends, and prevents her from earning a living. The purpose of such behavior, he explained, is to force her to become totally dependent on him, emotionally and financially. Without a support system of her own, the husband is able to treat her like a slave, physically and emotionally abusing her at will. The wife eventually reaches such a weakened state that she has no emotional or physical reserves to draw on, and succumbs to the situation.

The psychologist went on to explain that husbands like Motti do not permit their wives to work in their professions precisely because this would give them a sense of self-worth. Yet, Motti still needs her income — so the solution is to send her out on the streets to beg. Thus he kills two birds with one stone: he receives a "good income" and he humiliates his wife to the extent that she is without a will of her own.

The psychologist then advised us to check out whether our daughter was being beaten as well — and our tears showed him that an investigation wasn't necessary. We told him about the blow she got in our house. We also described our efforts to convince her to get help. He told us that the first step in getting help must come from her — she has to want to get out of the situation.

I still tried to keep in touch with Naomi, but they were never home, it seemed. Concerned, I called Motti's parents and they told me that Motti and Naomi had moved to another city. Further inquiries revealed that they had sold their apartment and purchased a single-family home at the edge of a small, isolated village. My heart sank. Naomi's imprisonment was complete.

For a long time we had no further contact, or to be more precise, we had very little. The contact we had consisted of regards she would send us through friends who encountered her — begging at the gravesites of holy men, which drew many visitors. My husband could not bear the situation, and the thought that his daughter had become a beggar at holy sites led to such anguish that he suffered a heart attack. A relative who saw Naomi at a holy gravesite informed her, and she came to visit her father. Since then she has kept in sporadic contact with us.

Rabbi Walder, I know that most of the stories you read out have a happy ending. However, this story has no end.

We have married off three more children, who have established loving families, thank God. Naomi now has six children. I have difficulty sleeping because she is always on my mind. I think about how she may be being held against her will, and I wonder if she is being hurt. At the same time, I am unable to do anything to help her. I keep my anxieties to myself because I don't want to aggravate my husband's heart condition.

I recently went to get some counseling, for my anxiety and pain were becoming too much for me to bear. As I told the counselor my story, she said, "Tell me, is Naomi happy?" Seeing my expression, she quickly added, "Happiness is one of life's biggest riddles, you know. A happy person is one who considers himself to be happy. A wealthy person can suffer from depression, and a poor person can be cheerful and content. Some people need freedom, and others need to be controlled, to have their lives ruled by someone else."

I did not really understand what she was getting at. I asked her, "Are you telling me that there are people who enjoy suffering?"

"I am sure your daughter is suffering," she said, "but she also suffered before she got married. Don't misunderstand me — you were not the cause of her suffering! Naomi was suffering from Naomi. She could not come to terms with herself, and she hated herself and her whole life. It is common among adolescent girls who have low self-esteem (and it may have seemed to you that her self-esteem was too high, but surely it was not) to think that as soon as they leave home and become "independent," then everything will be wonderful.

Naomi knows that you know her from a period in her life that she wants to erase. You know her difficulties and her weaknesses, and *that* is why she wants no contact with you. You remind her of things she wants to forget. Her present situation is certainly a bad one too. In her own mind she is trapped between two bad situations."

The counselor concluded the meeting by advising me to maintain some form of contact with my daughter, so that if she ever comes to the conclusion that she will be better off without her husband, then at least she will know that she can return to her parents' home.

She then warned me not to immerse myself totally in Naomi's problems. She assured me that I have done what I could do. Now, I should let her get on with her own life, and I should get on with mine.

I have been fairly successful in taking this advice. *Baruch Hashem*, I have many reasons to be happy — I am enjoying my other children and grandchildren, who come to visit us regularly. I guess I have more or less come to terms with Naomi's situation.

Rabbi Walder, I have come to the end of my painful story. I know that there are many teenage girls among your listeners, and I hope they hear this. It is important that girls who think they are not given enough independence, know that sometimes their need for independence can turn them into slaves for the rest of their lives. Escaping from negative feelings does not automatically guarantee positive feelings. If you try to erase your past, you might end up killing your future.

Win or Lose

Dear Rabbi Walder,

I am married and study Torah full-time in a *kollel* in a small town in southern Israel. The following story is well-known locally, but I am writing it to you since I feel it is important that it reach a wide audience. It contains a very important moral lesson.

Many people share a common dream — the dream of becoming wealthy overnight by winning the State Lottery. I admit that I am one of those who has always filled out the lotto forms every week in the hope of winning. However, this hope is now accompanied by trepidation and I am sure many residents of my town feel the same way.

Over the last ten years, three residents of my town have won first prize in the lottery. All three invested their winnings in grandiose but dubious projects, and all three ended up bankrupt debtors and met terrible fates. If it were just the financial loss, then one could shrug it off, but all three also endured great suffering. One was involved in three serious automobile accidents, and he is now confined to a wheelchair. Another became ill with an incurable disease shortly after he won the lottery.

The third winner is the best-known of all of them, since he let his name be published in the newspaper. Yossi won the largest single prize in Israel's history.

As soon as his win was made public, and even before he actually received the money, the requests for help began to stream in. His wife began answering the phone with the words: "Welfare Department!"

Yossi owned a small textile factory and provided a good living for his family. However, the huge amount that he won simply went to his head — and he refused to listen to his friends' sound advice about what to do with the money. Instead, Yossi decided to invest his money in a health and fitness club and in various other local businesses with the aim of doubling or trebling his assets. At the time, any new local business venture was assumed to be one of Yossi's investments.

What can I tell you? Yossi became a very suspicious person and distanced himself from his long-time friends. He began to suspect everyone of only being interested in his money. He seemed to forget that they had been his friends long before he won the lottery. In their place, wealthier people began to hang around Yossi, but they were not true friends; they were the ones who were only interested in Yossi's money. His social life changed completely, one thing led to another, and it didn't take long before Yossi decided to leave his wife and children and move out of town. His family was devastated.

Only a few years after the big win, Yossi was forced to declare bankruptcy. He was left with huge debts he could not pay off. To add to his woes, a year ago he became ill with cancer, and despite all the treatments he underwent, he died last week.

An ordinary man who had lived a peaceful life, owned a modest factory, and enjoyed a happy family, left this world as a lonely pauper filled with disappointment and bitterness.

The story of Yossi had a major impact on the residents of my town. People now look at life differently — things are not always what they seem, and wealth does not guarantee happiness. We have to learn to be satisfied with what we have and not to always be looking to see what the neighbor has. It is just unfortunate that it takes tragedy to make people realize this truth.

Our Sages understood this in ancient times. In *Pirkei Avos* 4:1, we read: "Who is wealthy? He who is happy with his portion."

I have spent a lot of time this last week thinking about Yossi's last years, since his big win. Poor Yossi! He had seemingly reached the peak of success and fell to the depths of despair. His wealth led to his downfall.

Over the years, the State Lottery has advertised with the slogan "You need the lottery in life." After Yossi's story, I don't need the lottery — I just want life.

Mazal

Dear Rabbi Walder,
    I recently read a newspaper report about something that happened at a family *sheva berachos* celebration in Netanya. One of the guests opened a bottle of Coca Cola which had details of a special offer on the back of the label. When she peeled off the label she saw that her bottle was the winner — she had won a car! She cried out excitedly that she had won, but then the bride's father intervened and said that the car rightfully belonged to him since he was the host of the evening and had provided the drinks. The *simchah* ended in disagreement.

The guest went to the Coca Cola offices with the winning label and the bride's parents appealed to the courts to settle the dispute. The guest was prepared to compromise and accept half the value of the car, but the other party would not hear of any settlement and continued to claim that the car rightfully belonged to them. As things stand at the moment, the court ruled that the Coca Cola company is not permitted to present the guest with the car until a final decision is reached.

Rabbi Walder, I don't know what *da'as Torah* has to say in

such a case, but in my humble opinion, this woman rightfully deserves to win the car. It was her *mazal*. It was her good fortune to open the bottle, and had she not done so who knows if someone else would have noticed the offer? Probably the empty bottle would have been thrown away at the end of the evening. I don't know the bride's family personally, but if anyone who hears this letter read on your program does know them, I have advice for them, and that is why I am writing to you, Rabbi Walder. My advice is: Don't tempt fate. I'm not saying this for no reason. My personal experience has led me to believe that it is dangerous to try and fight fate.

My husband, Chaim, comes from a well-to-do family. He and his older brother, Meir, were the only children and his parents were getting on in years when we got married. Chaim and Meir looked after their parents in their old age and took care of their every need. People admired the devotion of these two sons to their parents, and the two brothers were very close to each other as well.

Everything changed, however, when their father passed away. The actual execution of the will and division of property was carried out very smoothly because my father-in-law had divided his assets equally between his two sons. However, in his list of instructions he had neglected to list his car — a luxury, limited-edition Mercedes.

Chaim suggested that they sell the car and divide the money equally between them. Meir, on the other hand, claimed that the car was rightfully his, since he was the firstborn son. Chaim did not accept this because the will clearly showed that their father intended both his sons to receive an equal share of his assets. Although he didn't take Meir to court to settle the matter, he flatly refused to relinquish ownership of the car to his brother. Their elderly mother didn't know what to do. She didn't want or need the car. In the end, Meir approached the *Beis Din* and asked them to declare him the rightful owner of the

Mercedes. Chaim retained Rabbi Segal, who had special training in this branch of Jewish law, to represent him in front of the
judges of the *Beis Din*.

Rabbi Segal listened to Chaim's side of the story and agreed
that according to the will it was obvious that the deceased
wished his assets to be divided equally between his two sons.
Rabbi Segal was convinced that Chaim was in the right and
that the *Beis Din* would rule in his favor.

At home, Chaim discussed his dilemma with me. On the
one hand he didn't look forward to facing his only brother in
front of the *Dayanim*, and yet he couldn't accept the fact that he
stood to lose a large sum of money because of his brother's in-
transigence. I really sympathized with my husband's predicament and I did not know what to advise him. It was hard to say
whether he should graciously forego the money or whether he
should fight the matter to the end.

The night before the case was to be heard, Chaim made a
decision. In the morning he called Rabbi Segal and informed
him that he had decided to withdraw the claim. If Meir really
wanted the Mercedes so badly, he said, then let him have it.
Rabbi Segal was disappointed at this turn of events and tried to
convince my husband to come to the *Beis Din*, but Chaim's
mind was firmly made up.

"Rabbi Segal, please convey my decision to Meir at the *Beis
Din* and tell him that he can have the car and I wish him *Mazal
Tov* and all the very best for the future." The sarcastic tone in
Chaim's voice did not go unnoticed.

Meir was delighted when he heard the news. The *Av Beis
Din* handed him the keys to the Mercedes, and Meir quickly
went to his mother's home, which was situated at the top of a
high hill and had a breathtaking view.

He went in to visit with his elderly mother, to inform her of
the final decision, and then went out to the garage. With great
excitement he put the keys in the ignition and turned on the

powerful engine of the coveted Mercedes. He drove out of the garage and headed for his own home, which was situated in the valley below.

Halfway down the hill, Meir lost control of the car, crashed straight into a telephone pole, and was killed instantly.

Rabbi Walder, this is my true story and when I think of the bride's family insisting on their right to that car, I am filled with a feeling of impending doom. I wish someone would tell them the story I have just written to you. I feel that it is absolutely forbidden to try and take away someone else's *mazal*. Sometimes fate turns out to be very cruel and good fortune turns out to be bad. So let's leave things as they are.

Uprooted

Dear Rabbi Walder,
    I would not classify myself as one of your typical listeners, since I am not religious. However, I am always interested in hearing the true stories of people's lives, and the lessons they have learned, that make up your program.

It wasn't an easy decision to write my personal story to you. I know that if I were to publish my story in the national press, it would make headline news. I chose to write to you, however, because none of my acquaintances listen to your program, and therefore no one will be able to identify me. I don't have the courage to be a national news item, and yet I feel the need to publish my story.

I am a forty-four-year-old woman who lives in the Tel Aviv area. I come from a well-to-do family. My father was a doctor and my mother held a senior management position in a national organization. I was the only child of older parents who had come to Israel from Europe. They were wonderful to me, and gave me everything parents can give: both materially and emotionally. Life was good. We traveled abroad twice a year, and they gave me the best education. There was nothing they wouldn't do for my well-being and my happiness. I grew up to be like my parents: quiet, decent, and cultured.

I didn't have any of the usual teenage problems; I was an obedient daughter and I had a close relationship with my parents. They were not the kind of people who displayed their feelings a lot, but in their own quiet way let me know that I was very much loved. When I finished high school, I went into the army, and afterwards I began my studies at university.

One hot summer day, I met one of my mother's friends in town, and we decided to have a cold drink together. The conversation drifted to my parents. This woman spoke very highly of my mother and then, without thinking, she uttered the sentence which would change my entire life: "How we admired your mother! She raised you with such love and devotion — as if she was your biological mother!"

I turned deathly pale, and could not utter a sound. I felt the world had stopped. I wanted to say that I was sure that I hadn't heard correctly, but no sound came out.

The poor woman realized that I had not been aware of what she had revealed, and she tried to explain it to me, but I could not absorb what she was saying.

I walked out of the café in a state of shock. I could not believe what had just happened, that at the age of twenty-three I had discovered by chance that I was adopted. The next few days were a blur for me, and my head spun with questions. I decided that I would have to confront my parents.

The next afternoon I went to my father's clinic and waited until the last patient had gone and the secretary had left for the day. Then I walked into my father's office. He greeted me happily. I looked at him and asked him gently, "Why didn't you tell me that I was adopted?"

My father's face turned from white to red and back to white.

It took him a few moments before he could reply, and he spoke shakily:

"My dear daughter, my only daughter, your mother and I always intended to tell you the truth, but we never found the appropriate time. When you were little it didn't seem right, when you were in high school we put it off, and then we decided to wait until you finished your army service. Since then, every day we have decided to tell you, but we just didn't know how to do it."

Then for the first time ever, I saw my father cry. I told him that I understood their feelings, and indeed I did. I realized that my parents were such good people that they were not capable of telling me something like this that could be devastating for me. I reassured my father that I understood. At home I had a similar conversation with my mother. I tried to put it all "aside," but questions began to surface: Who am I? Who are my real parents? Why did they abandon me?

When I tried to get the information from my parents, they told me that they didn't know the answers and suggested that I go to the Welfare Service and open up the adoption file. But I didn't run to do this. I was too frightened to do anything that would alter the fabric of my life so much. Did I really want to know? Who were these "parents" who would give up a baby? My imagination ran wild and I began to think about violent, criminal characters who could be my parents. I didn't want to discover the truth. So I didn't try.

I finished my university studies, found a good job, got married, and then divorced. The fact is that since my discovery, I never felt at peace with myself. Not knowing my true identity made me feel I had no roots, and I felt I had lost all sense of belonging.

At one point I went for psychological counseling, and the therapist convinced me of the need to discover my true background so that I could make a real decision whether to contact my biological family or not. If I didn't come to terms with my past, if there were no "closure," I would not be able to build a stable future, she told me.

I decided to take her advice, and full of trepidation, I made an appointment with a social worker at the Welfare Services Department. She listened to me, offered me emotional support, and following some bureaucratic procedures, handed me my adoption file. Heart pounding, I read that my biological parents lived in a small town in southern Israel and that I was forcibly taken from them, against their will. A court order had been issued that I be put up for adoption because I was a neglected child.

I felt as if I had received a physical blow. I was a refined, cultured, respectable young woman — how could I have been a neglected child from a development town? The file also contained a letter to me written by my mother! She wrote:

To my dear daughter:

I want you to know that I didn't neglect you. It was all a plot by the authorities to steal you away from me. If you ever contact me I will tell you the truth.

I could tell from the handwriting and the spelling mistakes that she was not well-educated.

I put the file down and held my head in my hands. Who was this woman? I hated her because she couldn't write a letter without mistakes! I hated myself for being connected to some primitive woman! I hated the world in general. My self-esteem was shattered, and I felt utterly worthless.

I looked at the social worker. "Thank you very much for the information, but I will not be using it. I am not interested in having any contact with this woman."

"That is your choice," she replied, "and I won't put pressure on you. However, I do think that if you have already found the courage to open your adoption file, then you owe it to yourself to meet your biological mother at least once and find out exactly what happened when you were taken away from her."

"No!" I cried. "What if she clings to me and doesn't leave me alone to live my own life?" I knew I was being irrational. In my mind, I already pictured my "mother" as some kind of disgusting, penniless woman who would want to move into my house and my life.

The social worker nodded. "Well then, I have another suggestion," she said gently. "Will you give me permission to contact her and try and set up a meeting? I won't tell her where you live, and of course I will not divulge your name. Thus you will be able to cut off all contact with her after the first meeting, if you so desire."

"I don't know! Please give me a few days to think about your suggestion. I need time to come to a decision."

A few days later, after much agonizing, I gave my consent to the social worker to contact my biological mother. Within a few hours she called me back: "I have just spoken to your mother and she was utterly shocked by the news that you wanted to meet her. She almost fainted with excitement." That fit the image I'd developed of this primitive, neglectful woman. "She agreed to any conditions you wish to set," she went on, "as long as she gets to see you, even one time. I have set up the meeting at her home. Your biological father will be there too. Please take the address and phone number. I offer you my best wishes and support for the meeting."

I decided to go by taxi so that "my parents" would not be able to trace my identity through my car's license plates.

I traveled south to the small town and arrived at a single-story home which had been extended several times. I studied the house with a critical eye — its owners had put a lot of money into it, but they had not employed the services of an architect to plan the house properly.

I went up to the door and rang the bell. My mother looked

exactly as I had imagined her — a stooped, wrinkled woman, who looked like she'd had a hard life. She was probably a lot younger than she looked. My father wore a kind of cap on his head. Were they religious? He was missing some of his teeth. I went in, dazed, and we sat and stared at each other. Then my mother embraced me, and I had to gently disentangle myself from her.

We sat in awkward silence for a few more minutes, and then my parents began to cry. I also shed some tears. They were crying tears of joy and excitement, but my tears were tears of pain. I was facing two people who had been dreaming about me all their lives, and I felt I could not make any connection with them at all. I had nothing in common with these "parents."

Shortly after my arrival, three young men came to the house — my "brothers." They were tall, well-built men who were kind and friendly, but did not give the impression of being very refined people. They came with their wives, who spoke to me as if they had known me forever, all the time touching and kissing me. Someone put on some loud, Middle-Eastern music, and before long I had become the main attraction of a family celebration. Then the neighbors came in, without knocking on the door, to join in the celebration. I was numb. They all fit the stereotype I had of "lower class" Sephardim in a development town! What was I doing there?

My three brothers ran successful businesses. The oldest one owned a metal factory; the next brother ran a successful wedding hall; and the youngest brother owned a store of some kind.

According to the standards of the social circles I moved in, success was measured in terms of academic degrees. However, the world I was visiting judged success differently, and my brothers were certainly success stories in their world.

I should point out that they were all extremely kind to me and tried to ignore the fact that I looked and sounded so differ-

ent from them. They quickly caught on to the distances between us, and they seemed somewhat disappointed. I clearly
wasn't "one of them" — although I did resemble them physically. To their credit, they were all very polite despite the fact
that I was so unresponsive. Eventually my brothers left with
their wives, not before we had another round of kisses.

The neighbors left too.

My father seemed too overwhelmed to sit and talk to me
and went to lie down.

Left alone with my mother, I asked her, in a delicate way,
what had happened.

She cried as she began to speak. "They stole you away from
me, my baby! I tried to speak to all the social workers, but no
one believed me. I didn't want them to take you away from me,
but the authorities were too powerful. One day they came to
my house, with policemen, and just took you away. We cried
all night. I will never, ever forgive them!"

"But what reason did they give for taking me away?" Of
course I had read the word "neglected" in my adoption file, but
I wanted to hear from my mother.

"They accused me of neglecting you. It was simply not true!
I loved you and pampered you like all my other children. But
you had a problem. You vomited everything you ate. I took
you to doctors, and to rabbis for blessings, all over the country.
We were always on buses, going everywhere I heard about
someone who might help. Nothing helped — you continued to
vomit all the time. By the time you reached the age of
one-and-a-half, you were so thin, really undernourished, and
it's true, you *looked* as if I were neglecting you! They didn't
want to know that it wasn't my fault. I did everything I could,
and followed all the advice I was given, but nothing helped.
Nothing."

Listening to her, I suddenly understood what had happened. To this day I suffer from celiac disease. I am allergic to

gluten and cannot eat any food containing wheat flour. I have learned to live with my condition. My adoptive parents told me that as a child I was constantly throwing up, and that my father went abroad to seek advice from world-renowned experts, until finally one specialist made the diagnosis of celiac disease. As soon as they changed my diet, my problems disappeared immediately, and I began to grow and thrive like any normal child.

The truth was overwhelming! My poor mother had not neglected me — she did exactly what my adoptive father had done — she too went from doctor to doctor seeking help, but no one was able to provide an answer. Who knows, if I had been kept in my mother's care, some doctor would eventually have reached the correct diagnosis. And I would have stayed with my biological family.

My mother poured her heart out to me, reliving the terrible thing that had been done to her. "I will never forget the shame they brought on me by accusing me of neglecting you. Look at your brothers — do they look as if they were neglected? They lacked nothing and neither did you. But the authorities didn't believe me. They thought because we were poor, that we were "primitive" and didn't know how to raise our children... but you must understand — you were not neglected!"

"I believe you," I said. "I know you were not guilty of neglect."

Then I felt I had to leave. I told her I was going. "Please, I beg you!" she cried. "Don't just disappear from my life now that you've come back. I've dreamt about you every night. Even if you don't want to visit again, at least keep in touch with me by mail."

"I promise to keep in touch with you," I said.

The visit ended and I rode home in a turmoil. I could not sleep that night. I relived the entire visit and tried to come to terms with the meeting. Who was I? My two families were as different from each other as they could be.

The following morning I confronted my parents with a question that had haunted me all night: "Why didn't you try to cancel the adoption and give me back to my biological parents as soon as you discovered my celiac disease? Surely you must have realized that I wasn't neglected, and that this was the whole reason they took me away and put me up for adoption."

"We knew nothing about your biological parents," my mother said.

"No one ever told us that your mother had been accused of neglecting you," my father added. "We adopted a very sick child, and your condition deteriorated when you first came to us. We spared no effort or cost to try and find a cure for you. We just assumed that your biological parents had willingly given you up for adoption because they could not cope with your problems."

"Look at the situation from our point of view," my mother said. "We adopted a very sick baby whose parents, we assumed, could not take care of her."

I saw that my parents were crushed by my accusation. But I was overwhelmed with a storm of emotions.

"But look. I was sick when I was with my biological mother, and I was sick when you adopted me — and my condition even deteriorated when I first came to you! But *you* were never accused of neglecting me, no social worker tried to take me away from *you*, and the authorities wouldn't dream of accusing *you* of neglecting me."

By now I was crying. "Do you know why? Because you are respectable professional people, from the correct background and social status, from Europe. No one would suspect you of neglecting your children! My poor mother, who went from one doctor to another seeking help, who had limited financial means and no emotional support from anybody — she wasn't judged by the same criteria you were! It was assumed that because she was an immigrant from a backward village in Morocco, then the obvious explanation for my condition was maternal neglect. And a great injustice was done to her. She was left alone to mourn for her lost child and to face the scorn of her neighbors. I was taken away under police escort! How could they be so cruel to my mother? Oh, do you realize what they did to her?"

At this point, I was really breaking down. And I looked at my elderly parents and saw tears were streaming down their cheeks as well.

"My dear," my father began, searching for words. "Please believe us, we always have and always will want only the best for you. We fully understand your anger and what you are going through. Please don't accuse us, however. We only wanted the best for you."

Then my mother made a suggestion which must have been terribly painful for her. "Perhaps you'd like to move to your biological parents' town and try and rebuild a relationship with them?" Her voice trembled.

"I don't think I can," I wept. "The gap between my world and theirs is too wide."

At that moment I grasped the full extent of my predicament. I had been taken from my biological parents — and they had been taken from me. I was born into a religious, loving, warm, and simple family and was forcibly disconnected from my natural milieu. I was raised with love and security, true, but as a secular, cultured, somewhat cold, snobbish person. I was cut off from any threads that could possibly tie me to my biological parents.

I realized then and there that I would never be able to feel true peace and happiness again, that there was nowhere I truly belonged.

This feeling of not belonging to anything or anybody intensified, and my emotional state deteriorated. My adoptive parents sent me for psychological counseling, but this didn't help me much.

I came to wish that I had never discovered that I was adopted, or that I had known about it from an early age.

A few years later I remarried. My husband has been a wonderful pillar of support for me with this problem. I did not sever my relationship with my biological mother. We would meet in a café from time to time. I never divulged my name to her. She always brought me basketfuls of her homemade delicacies, and I always felt slightly embarrassed to be seen sitting with her. I felt that our meetings were more for her sake than for mine, and that I was doing a kind of mitzvah by agreeing to meet her. I did not want any contact with my brothers — I just did not know how to handle it, and I could not relate to my biological father, and so I never went to their house.

Last year my biological father passed away and my husband and I attended the funeral: During the course of the *levayah*, I made a spur-of-the-moment decision to stay with my mother during the *shivah*. My husband went home to bring some clothes for me, and I was given the guest-room in my mother's house for the whole week of mourning. My brothers sat up late every night. I would hear them talking and laughing together, reliving old memories, and occasionally I even joined them and tried to learn more about my family. To my pleasant surprise, I actually started to feel some kind of connection with them during the *shivah*. I would go so far as to say that I started liking them. They are very kind and loving. At the same time, they are very forthright people. They say exactly what they think, flare up quickly and then immediately make up. They are so different from the people I grew up with, went to school with, and worked with, who are polite and cold to each other by comparison.

During the *shivah*, I discovered the bond of a close-knit family, which I rejected and at the same time was jealous of — I wanted it too, in a way. My sisters-in-law included me in all their conversations. They were accustomed to discussing problems which affected individual family members, in the wider family forum. I found that amusing, but I also liked it.

At the end of the *shivah* week, we followed the custom of going to my father's grave. My brothers seemed to be recovering from the shock of his death, but I, who had hardly known this reticent stranger, approached the grave with a wave of emotions that I had been holding back. I cried for everything that had happened to me, for my parents — all four of them — and for me. My brothers stood around embarrassed, not quite knowing what to do with me — they only knew me as being so reserved. My sisters-in-law tried to hold me and calm me down, but it didn't help — my tears would not stop flowing.

Here at my father's grave, I felt for the first time part of my biological family. When my mother embraced me, I finally felt able to embrace her in return.

They now know my name, and I visit them several times a year. During my visits, I feel like a relative who has come from abroad — happy to see them, connected to them, but — still "other."

Rabbi Walder, I have come to the end of my story, and I want to conclude with a heartfelt plea to the adoption authorities. I do not deny that in certain cases adoption is a necessary procedure in order to guarantee the welfare of the child. And I realize that procedures are different today. But still, I wish to stress, in the strongest possible language, the absolute necessity of checking and double-checking every aspect of the case before initiating adoption procedures. It is imperative to consider whether preconceived notions and stereotyped images are hindering objective assessment of the case. I very strongly recommend that you first consider every other available option besides adoption. For example, it is possible for a child to be placed with a foster family, even temporarily, and still retain contact with his biological parents.

The most important recommendation I have is based on my own unhappy experience. I beg of you not to uproot a person from his ethnic background. There should always be the option for him to reconnect with his biological family, even after many years of separation. He should never have to "look down" on his parents and their ethnic background just because he was brought up in different surroundings. A person who is uprooted from his natural milieu will remain essentially rootless forever.

I Love You, Mommy

Dear Rabbi Walder,

I would never have thought about writing my life story to you if I hadn't heard the story on your program last week about a woman who was taken away from her biological parents at a young age, and adopted.

I heard her very critical comments about adoption agencies and the ease with which children have been taken away from their parents because of alleged negligence, as in her case, and put up for adoption. And I decided that you should hear another story about this subject.

My name is Esther. I was also born in a small town in southern Israel. I was a lively, friendly, and cheerful young girl who had many friends. I didn't get along well with my parents, though, and I was too influenced by others.

At the tender age of seventeen I went against my parents' wishes and married my boyfriend, a young man as immature as I was. The marriage lasted exactly two years and ended when my husband gave me a *get* and left me with two mementos — our one-year-old son and the unborn baby I was carrying.

I gave birth one month after the divorce. Reality hit me that at the grand old age of nineteen-and-a-half, I was responsible for two infants, without any support from my family. You see, I had broken off contact with my parents when I got married, and now my pride would not allow me to go back to them, certainly not to beg for their help.

Even now, so many years later, when I look back at that period of my life, I feel on the verge of tears. It is difficult for me to describe the living nightmare my life had become. When I was released from the hospital, I was physically exhausted and penniless. I didn't even have money for diapers for my newborn son, and I did not know whom to call for assistance. I was too proud to even try to find out. Luckily, good neighbors helped me somewhat. I was barely functioning, trying to care for my newborn, Ariel, and my one-year-old, Koby. I did not know how to deal with Koby's jealousy at all.

In fact, I simply did not know what to do. My days were a blur of feeding, changing, and bathing two babies. Even though I would make myself sing and laugh with them, inside I felt weak and incapable, alone and frightened. Just thinking about those days makes me feel weak, physically and emotionally! My maternal instincts forced me to take care of my sons — but there was no one to take care of me!

My situation worsened as I ran out of the little money I had. At that time my parents heard of my plight and they came to help. When they arrived I didn't have the strength to put on a brave face; I simply collapsed into bed and stayed there for a few days! My mother was a great help. She bought baby clothes, blankets, and a heater for the apartment. However, as soon as my strength returned, our old tensions flared up again. I resented her trying to tell me what to do. (I suppose that was the reason I had wanted to leave home at such a young age in the first place.) Once again we went our separate ways, though this time we did not lose contact completely.

I found a job, which made me feel good, but half my salary went to a babysitter. I would come home from work tired and irritable, play with my sons and read them stories, and then take them out to the playground. I did everything without any real enthusiasm, however. I was like a person carrying around a heavy load who could only think about how good it would be to get rid of that load. There were times I felt I'd gone from being a young girl to an old woman with nothing in between.

I was able to support us with my salary. Koby and Ariel were not easy children, however; they were lively and full of energy. I had to deal with complaints from the neighbors and from my children's nursery school teachers. I never argued with the teachers or tried to defend my sons, but on the other hand I didn't punish them either — I simply didn't have the energy!

When Koby started school, the principal insisted that a social worker be appointed to "supervise" me. Ella was her name. I hated her from the start, because as far as I could see, she didn't help me at all — she only told me what to do! She was very condescending, which made me even angrier. She even hinted that my children might be better off with "opportunities" I couldn't give them.

One day Koby told me that Ella had taken photographs of the walls in our living room when I wasn't there, and after that I told her not to come back. I realized that Ella intended to give a negative report about me.

To be honest, I could understand why the walls would be really appalling to her, and I'll tell you why. I let Koby and Ariel draw all over the walls without limits. They loved it, and I didn't see why I should tell them to stop! Also I realized that it was an outlet for their energies. A visitor might have thought the house looked neglected because of the state of the walls, but I never felt that way. (I even liked them a little.) And I was glad the children had a way to let off steam.

The local welfare department got involved and sent over an

"official" to have a look. Mrs. Roth was very nice but she hinted that I had should exert more control over my children and improve the state of my house. She even said they would give me money for painting the walls. Initially I agreed, but then my stubborn streak got the better of me and I told her I didn't want a painter to come and destroy my children's drawings. However, I said, I would ask my sons, and they would have the final word.

Koby and Ariel agreed with me that they didn't want to have their pictures painted over, with the exception of one wall which was moldy from dampness. When Mrs. Roth left the house, I could tell that she thought we were all crazy. When she left, Koby and Ariel started laughing and I joined in. Still, underneath my laughter I recognized despair. What was I doing to my children?

I was called in to meet with Koby's principal several times a week to discuss his behavior. At the end of the year, he was asked to leave that school, and Ariel, who would be starting first grade, was refused acceptance! As if things were not bad enough, I was fired from my job. Then I got sick! To top things off, one of my neighbors knocked on my door that night and angrily informed me that if I could not control my children, he would find a way to do so.

This was the "straw that broke the camel's back." That night the boys were really being difficult and wouldn't go to bed. When they finally went to sleep, I sat on my bed crying and crying. I felt the weight of all my problems was too much for my shoulders to bear. Where would I send them to school? Who would take them? Why were they so hard to manage? What would I do for our livelihood? And I was sick! I felt that there was no point in living, that nothing positive would ever come out of my life.

I took out an old photo album from my high-school days, and as I looked at the pictures of myself a few short years earlier, I cried bitter tears. I thought back to those days when I was the happiest girl in my class. And now? My life seemed a failure. A dead end.

I thought of Koby and Ariel and I couldn't decide who was worse off — them or me. They had to live without a father and with a mother who hated her life. And what kind of life was I giving them?

Rabbi Walder, it is not easy for me to say this, but at that point I also felt sorry for myself. I felt that they kept *me* from living, too.

After a sleepless night I made a drastic decision. First thing in the morning I contacted Ella, the social worker who had given a negative report on me and hinted that my children might have to be taken into foster care.

"Ella," I told her, "I have been thinking about what you said, and I have come to believe that my children *would* be better off if they were with a foster family. I am not coping — financially or emotionally. Of course I would want to see them often, but if you think that they would have a better life if they were adopted — then so be it." I was shocked by my own words, but I meant them. It was despair speaking.

"Well," she replied, "I'm certainly surprised by your readiness, Esther. I will forward your application to the appropriate channels."

I waited a month or so and then I was summoned, together with Koby and Ariel, to be assessed by a psychologist at City Hall. I didn't give the children any details — I simply told them that someone wanted to speak to us. We were with the psychologist for about five hours, and she spoke to us separately and together, and gave us all a battery of tests.

For three weeks, I waited tensely for the results. Then I was summoned to a new social worker who worked for the foster-care services. I was asked to come without the children.

My heart was pounding as I entered her office and sat down

on the edge of the chair. Nechama was a kind and gentle woman, about forty-five years old. She looked at me and smiled. Then she quietly informed me that the psychologist who had assessed us had recommended that the children stay with me.

I was stunned, and began to shout at her. "You social workers are always against the people you're supposed to help! When parents fight for their children, you want to take them away, but when I ask you to take them so they can have a good life, then you decide that I should keep them! Are you just being spiteful? Don't you care about my children?"

Nechama listened without saying a word, and then offered me a cold drink. "I read the psychologist's report, Esther — and I became your number one admirer."

"What?" I stared at her.

She smiled again. "I want to break one of my professional rules and let you see part of the psychologist's report. Look here — she wrote that your children have above-average intelligence, that they are unusually articulate and artistic, and that their self-confidence is far more developed than most children of their age. The report contained examples of the boys' comments to prove just how mature and articulate they really are."

I could not speak. Nechama then turned to the part of the assessment that dealt with me. I was described as a person who is physically and mentally exhausted, who does not think she is fit and deserving to bring up her own children. However, the report continued, there was a difference between my perceptions of myself and my actual behavior with my sons. The report stated that in reality I devoted my entire life to my children, and in my own way give them warmth, love, confidence, and happiness. The psychologist rejected Ella's recommendations.

Nechama categorically insisted on leaving the children in my care, because, she told me, I provided a warm, loving atmosphere which offers the children emotional and intellectual stimulation. She added that the psychologist did recommend that I attend some counseling sessions to boost my self-confidence and my "battered maternal identity" (this is a quote from the report which I have kept since then). The report stated that my biggest problem was that I didn't believe in myself and did not realize how much I have given to my children.

I continued to sit in stunned silence.

"My dear, I have studied your file in detail. Everything I read, including the criticism of you as a mother, caused me to admire you. Can you guess what made the biggest impression on me?"

I shook my head.

Without a word, Nechama opened my file and showed me the photographs that Ella had taken of the walls in my house — the walls that were covered with Koby and Ariel's drawings.

At first I thought she was making fun of me, but to my surprise I saw tears in her eyes. That was the last thing I expected from a social worker!

"I doubt if you were consciously aware of your actions, but you are blessed with inner joy, Esther, and creativity — and your sons absorbed these things. Your ability to let them develop their personalities, each one in his own special way, is amazing. You offered them support and warmth, despite the fact that you didn't receive much during your own childhood. You have great inner strengths."

Nechama's words touched me immensely, and my tough exterior crumbled. I began to cry. Could it be that this was happening? That someone thought I was such a good person? That someone actually admired me? *Me?*

"My dear," she went on, "I would like to be personally in charge of your case, and I promise never to give you orders telling you what to do."

"Nechama, I don't know if I can trust a social worker, even a special one like you."

"Look, Esther, I was able to discern things in these pictures of the walls that even you, their mother, didn't see. Isn't that enough of a reason for you to trust me?"

It was.

Nechama and I quickly became close friends. She was true to her word, and she never told me what to do. She arranged tutoring for my sons and sessions with the counselor at their school. She also arranged for me to have vocational testing and then enroll in a course for medical secretaries, so that I would be able to get a decent job. In short, Nechama instilled a new spirit in me.

Gradually she began to tell me details of her own life. It turned out that she was not married, and she had given up all hope of finding a suitable husband. It was an *eye-opener* to me that there were people who were worse off than I was, even though judging by appearances they seemed to have every-thing. Nechama's childhood had been carefree. She had ex-celled in school, and she had two degrees in psychology, but still she had never experienced real happiness. We spent many hours comparing notes on our lives and talking about how both of us had suffered in the past, in different ways. Nechama taught me to like myself, to get back in touch with my cheerful nature.

When I finished my course I got a new job — as a medical secretary. I really enjoyed my work. Koby and Ariel became changed children, and I learned to be proud of them. In many ways I didn't act like a typical mother. For instance, I had a golden rule that I would never rebuke my children for a fault that I myself had! If they were ever dishonest, though, I permit-ted myself to tell them off, because I considered honesty to be one of my strong points. My sons knew how much I loved them and that I would always be there for them, whatever problems they had. They knew that I really believed in them. And they believed in themselves.

At the age of thirty, I was offered a *shidduch* with a recently widowed, wealthy businessman. Initially, I balked at hearing the word "widower." He sounded so old, but it turned out that Asher was only five years older than I was. He was quite different from me in personality, but opposites attract and we liked each other from the first date. When I realized it was serious, I asked Koby and Ariel if they agreed to my remarriage and they were enthusiastic. Asher and I were married a short time later.

What can I say? Life became glorious. Although I had been on the right track for several years, for the first time I was treated like a queen. Asher is a very special and considerate person. He went out of his way to shower my children with love — and they returned his love. My friendship with Nechama continued, even though I officially didn't need her help any more, material or emotional.

During the years that followed, Asher and I were blessed with two daughters and a son. My previous sorrows were gone forever, in every way.

One day Nechama called me with the news that because of municipal cutbacks, she had been asked to leave her job and take early retirement.

For the first time in my life, I used my "connections." I told Asher that I literally owed my life to Nechama, and I asked him to pull every possible string at City Hall. It took him two days, but in the end he succeeded.

Nechama returned to her job as a social worker, but something had changed in her. I realized that she had become embittered with life. Now the tables were turned and I found myself trying to comfort and encourage her.

I was a young, wealthy woman who had everything to live for, and she was a sad, lonely, older woman without family who despaired of the future.

At first I was uncomfortable with this reversal of our roles, and I didn't know how to help a woman who was so much older than I was. But then I thought about our first meeting many years before, when it was I who was hopeless. Single-handedly she had lifted me up from the depths of despair and given me hope. Because of Nechama I became what I am today. Now was the time to repay her for everything she had done for me.

I told Nechama that I wanted her to become an "honorary grandmother" to Koby and Ariel, and to my children from my marriage to Asher. We invited her for Shabbos, Festivals, and to all our *simchas* and family gatherings. She developed a close relationship with my children, which gave her *nachas*.

Koby and Ariel are both married now and have set up true Jewish homes with their wonderful wives. They are devoted sons as well. I thank Hashem every day for the good He has bestowed on me and I am truly grateful for my wonderful life. The difficult years have enabled me to appreciate what I have now.

Rabbi Walder, I have reached the end of my story. I want your listeners to hear about how wonderful social workers can be. Some people may think that they spend their time trying to take children away from their parents! But they sometimes exert all their power to keep children *with* their parents, no matter what. In my case, Nechama helped me see the good when I could only see the bad in myself and in my life. She saved my life. She was a messenger sent by Hashem.

Six months ago, at Ariel's wedding, I was surprised when Nechama handed me an envelope. I opened it and stared. With trembling hands I took out a faded photograph of a wall — a wall covered with pictures in many colors, with red sheep and blue houses, with purple flowers and green people. Scrawled in childish handwriting were the words: *I love you, Mommy.*

Tears sprang to my eyes and I felt all my makeup smudge, but I was too overcome with emotion to care. I truly owed my very life to Nechama.

Lost and Found

Dear Rabbi Walder,

Although I have been living in New York for many years, I still manage to listen to your program, along with many other former Israelis who live here. The story I want to tell you happened to me over twenty years ago, when I was newly married and still lived in Israel.

I had always had a good voice and from the time I was a child, I performed in public — at family gatherings, special events, and various other forums. At some point I decided to sing professionally, and I became a popular and well-known singer. I don't know if you ever heard of me — Itzik Levy.

When I got married at the age of twenty-two, my future seemed bright. And when my repertoire reached ten original songs, I took the advice many people had given me and I decided to produce a cassette of my own songs.

You can't imagine what went into the production of a cassette then, Rabbi Walder. I hired a well-known producer and top musicians for the sound track, and we started recording. I didn't cut any corners to achieve top-notch quality — I put my heart and soul into this project, as I sincerely believed it would be a commercial success and establish me as a top singer.

I took out loans to cover the high production costs and I was certain that I'd have no problem repaying them from sales profits. This portion of the project dragged out over six months because of various problems — budgetary and technical — and then the next stage was to record me singing the songs backed by the recording made by the orchestra. This stage took another two months, and there were lots of delays here too: my reserve duty in the army; a bad throat infection; my producer's other commitments; and more.

Finally, the recording was completed. With a sense of joy and relief, I received the huge recording tapes. I loaded them into my car and set off for Herzliya, where the tapes would be transformed into cassettes. As I turned the key in the ignition, I suddenly remembered that I'd forgotten some bourekas in the studio — I'd bought them for supper earlier. So I turned off the engine, ran up to the studio, grabbed the bag of bourekas, and ran out again to the car.

The car! Where was it? It wasn't where I thought I'd parked it! Thinking that I must have forgotten exactly where I'd parked it, I ran around the block looking for my car. After five minutes of frantic searching, the bitter truth hit me. Someone had stolen my car. I couldn't have cared less about my old car — the insurance would pay for a new one — but the contents, my precious tapes, were in the car and now they were gone! I was distraught beyond words and beside myself with fear and apprehension.

I called the police to report the theft, and I broke down in tears on the phone and begged the clerk to give an order to set up roadblocks. He burst out laughing and said that the police weren't in the habit of setting up roadblocks to search for old, stolen cars. When I went in person to the police station and begged them to do something to help me, they told me that the chances of recovering a stolen car were virtually nil. They did agree to search for it and its precious contents, however.

I trudged back on foot to the studio and asked if they had a copy of my recordings. They said no. I felt like I'd been dealt a physical blow. The full extent of my loss sank in.

I did not despair easily. I put notices in local newspapers asking the thief to return the contents of the car and no further questions would be asked. But to no avail — the thief obviously didn't see the ads or didn't care.

I was traumatized. I felt my life was ruined. I can't explain it, but I lost my touch for singing too. I think I lost faith in myself and did not believe that I would see any results from further efforts. I was also suffering from "burnout." I'd invested so much physical and emotional effort, not to mention borrowed money, into the project and now I no longer had the strength to start all over again.

I still sang at weddings in order to make a living, but my heart wasn't in it. I simply could not come to terms with what had happened, and I was faced with heavy debts which I couldn't repay. My love of singing faded away.

I felt I needed to make a clean break and a new start, so my wife and I moved to New York. Life was very tough and I barely eked out a living from odd jobs which were totally unconnected to music. I'd always heard that America was the land of unlimited opportunities, but I soon discovered that it was also the land of unlimited poverty. I was used to Israel with its national insurance benefits, but in America it's not so easy, and if you're penniless you're worthless. It took ten long years until I finally had a good, permanent job and was able to make a decent living. In those years our five wonderful children were born. They gave us no end of joy and made the difficult times easier to bear.

Seven years ago I started working in hi-tech, and thank God I was very successful. I finally fulfilled the American dream. The difficult years were now behind us and I felt secure. The downturn in the hi-tech industry only affected me marginally. Rabbi

Walder, if that were the end of my story I don't think I'd be writing to you. The last chapter in this twenty-two-year-old story took place two months ago.

Out of the blue, I got a phone call from the man who produced my recordings back then. "Itzik?" he said. "Are you sitting down? Take a deep breath." This is what he told me:

"Listen, Itzik, I've been in the same studio all these years, and last week, I moved to a new, larger one. When I was packing up the old studio, I came across a large collection of old demo tapes which had been in a dusty storeroom for years. I was curious and decided to listen to some of these. The music was vaguely familiar but I couldn't figure out who the singer was. I listened to the songs over and over again, trying to remember who it was, and suddenly it hit me: it was you, Itzik! I vividly recalled your story and what had happened to your tapes. I have no idea why I'd made copies, and how somehow another singer's name got put on them."

"Well," I said, when I could speak. "This is quite a shock. Can you please make another copy and send it to me by courier? Don't worry about the cost, you can bill me."

The tapes arrived within 24 hours. In a wave of nostalgia, I went into my study and turned it on. The once familiar music took me back twenty years, and I thought about all the good and bad things that had happened to me in that time.

I recalled how I was as a young man, full of energy and optimism for the future, how I started climbing the ladder of success as a professional singer. Then I remembered how Hashem suddenly threw me off that ladder, in a very painful way, and took away my opportunity and my enthusiasm for continuing on my chosen path.

I grieved a lot over my loss, but deep down I have known for many years that Hashem was actually being kind to me, Rabbi Walder. When I am honest with myself, I admit that becoming a singer wasn't really the right path for me. I wouldn't have been very successful. I might have put out a number of cassettes, but I would never have become first-class. And the life that comes with being a professional entertainer — who knows what effect it could have had on my children, and what kind of childhood they would have had?

I've come to the conclusion that what at the time seemed like a tragedy, was actually a blessing in disguise from Hashem. Then, I was angry and bitter, but I have since discovered that you have to thank Hashem for the bad in the same way as you thank Him for the good. I might add that what initially *seems* bad, is ultimately good.

Dangerous Game

Dear Rabbi Walder,
My wife and I feel as if we have been living through a high-suspense thriller for the past few months. Yet this is no story, unfortunately — every word is true and it does not have a happy ending.

Esty and I have been married for five years and we have not yet been blessed with children. About a year after our marriage, our family and friends began to ask us discreetly if everything was all right. Of course we realized that everything was not all right, and we began to deal with the problem on every level. I cannot tell you how many times we have visited the graves of *tzaddikim* to pour out our hearts, or how many prominent Rabbis have given us a blessing. We went from one medical specialist to the next, and there is almost no fertility treatment that we haven't tried. You can imagine the emotional stress that we went through — and all to no avail.

Then four months ago we were given the most wonderful news possible. Words cannot describe the happiness and thankfulness we felt when we were told that we would soon become parents. Our lives were full of joy — until that fateful

171

phone call which heralded the onset of our nightmare.

I came home from *kollel* for lunch as usual, looking forward to spending a peaceful hour with Esty. I was shocked to find her trembling, and as white as a sheet. She could hardly utter a sound; she just pointed to the phone and told me to listen to the message. I rushed to turn on the answering machine.

The message began with the sound of gunshots, and then a menacing voice said: "We are going to get you — and that will be the end of you!" I was also shocked at first, but then I took charge of the situation and tried to reassure Esty that someone was surely playing a practical joke on us. It took me a long time to calm her down, and when I went back to *kollel* for the afternoon study session, Esty insisted on spending the afternoon at her parents' house, as she was too frightened to stay alone. On my way home from *kollel* in the evening I picked her up, and was happy to see that she felt better.

That night we were awakened from a sound sleep by the shrill ring of the telephone at midnight. As I lifted the receiver, I heard the voice again: "Good night, Tzvi and Esty." Then the line went dead. With trembling hands I put down the phone. This nightmare was turning out to be an ongoing one. It wasn't the actual message that worried me; I just didn't know what to tell Esty. I decided to tell her that it was a wrong number but she knows me too well and she guessed that it was our mystery caller on the line. I was stupid enough to tell her that the caller had mentioned our names. Esty couldn't sleep the rest of the night, and at the slightest sound she sent me to the front door to check that nobody was there.

Our way of life changed. Esty refused to stay at home alone, so when I went to learn in the morning she went to her parents, and on my way home for lunch I would pick her up. More often than not, we would come home and find another frightening message on the answering machine. Although I tried to tell Esty that it was only a practical joker who was having some fun at our expense, she became convinced that there was someone out there who had a personal vendetta against me. Nothing I said could persuade her otherwise.

Our lives turned into a living nightmare. At least twice a week we would find a frightening message on the answering machine. Esty lost weight, and couldn't sleep at night. Nothing I said could calm her down. I decided to change our phone number and make the new number unlisted.

We then enjoyed a blissful few days of tranquility, but this turned out to be only a brief respite. A week after we changed the number, Esty answered the phone and heard the strange, now-familiar voice: "I have contacts everywhere, and they got me your new number. Tell Tzvi that no one can get away from me."

Esty slammed the phone down and collapsed onto the couch, crying. At that moment I was ready to strangle our tormentor — if only I could find him! How could someone have gotten our unlisted number?

We disconnected our telephone and bought a cellphone. Once again we had a peaceful respite. Esty began to sleep again and to become her normal, cheerful self. Unfortunately our happiness was short-lived.

One evening we were relaxing over a cup of coffee when the phone rang. Esty answered before I had a chance and pressed a few buttons to retrieve the text message. It read: "I know your address," and on the screen appeared a picture of a gun. We stared at it in stunned silence.

I now began to share Esty's fears. We were apparently being stalked by an enemy who really had contacts everywhere, which explained how he had gotten our cellphone number. I felt we no longer had control of our own lives, and the privacy of our home did not shelter us from our intruder.

We immediately called the police, but the receptionist answered in a bored voice that I should come in the morning, in person, to file a complaint.

I duly arrived at the police station the following morning and presented the details. I begged the police to trace all the calls made to my two previous phone numbers. The policeman informed me that they carry out such checks only if there is serious justification, but he said that if anything new turned up I should contact them again.

I went home and assured Esty that everything would be all right, that the police would find out the identity of our tormentor. She felt reassured and we had a quiet evening together and went to bed early. However, at midnight the phone rang. Esty answered it and heard the now-familiar voice: "We are coming to get you at four o'clock this morning." Then the line went dead.

Esty began to cry, and asked me to take her straight to her parents, which I thought was a good idea. But then she changed her mind and said she would stay at home because she didn't want to alarm them at such an hour. She remembered we had installed double locks both on the front door and on our bedroom door, and I tried again to convince her that this was just a practical joker.

We tried to go back to sleep but without much success. Unfortunately we had spent many such sleepless nights during the last two-and-a-half months. I must have dozed off around 2:00 AM.

Esty woke me urgently sometime later: she was having terrible pains.

"Don't worry, Esty," I said. "I'm sure it's only psychological."

"No, Tzvi! This is for real — I must be checked by a doctor. Please call an ambulance immediately."

Unfortunately, our visit to the hospital was a short and sad one. Esty had a miscarriage. Rabbi Walder, you cannot imagine how we felt. We had been childless for five years. For five long years we had waited to receive the wonderful news and now, because of an evil, heartless person our happiness was ruined. Pain, sorrow, loss and mourning welled up inside us and nothing could stop the flow of our tears.

The following morning I rushed over to the police station, and burst into the building shouting, "You told me to come back if anything happened — well, I'm back sooner than you thought, and something terrible happened. My wife lost our child because of this evil person." I couldn't go on. I was choked with tears.

The police were extremely sympathetic. They ignored my ranting and my tears and sat me down in a side room, offering me a cold drink. One particular policeman, Saul, was especially supportive and even shed a tear when I told him how much Esty and I had been suffering. He told me that nothing in the world would stop him now from finding our tormentor.

Two days later, Saul called and told me to come over to the station immediately because they had caught him. I ran out of the house, flagged down a taxi, and raced to the station. Saul told me the suspect was being interrogated and asked me to wait while he went to get permission for me to enter the room. The senior police officer came out of the room and whispered something to Saul, who looked at him with an amazed expression. I realized there had been some kind of breakthrough in the case. Saul sighed and told me to enter the room and see for myself who had been brought in for questioning.

I thought I was dreaming when I walked in and saw Davie, Esty's teenage brother, sitting in the center of the room. What was this kid doing here under questioning? Davie looked at me and said, "Come on, Tzvi, can't you guys take a joke? Why did you have to go to the police? Just get me released now."

This was too much for me. I lost control and started to hit him, calling him a child murderer and an evil person. Saul tried to separate us but it was no easy task and he had to call for help.

Saul asked if I wanted to withdraw the charges but I was not prepared to. I went home and gently revealed to Esty, who had just been released from the hospital, the identity of the anonymous caller who had ruined our lives. She shook her head in utter disbelief and we both cried bitterly.

Her parents and older siblings came to see us. They were shocked to hear of Davie's stupid pranks, which had led to such terrible consequences. My parents-in-law took me aside and asked me if I was prepared to withdraw the charges against him. They explained that he had been remanded in custody and he now fully understood the gravity of his actions. He hadn't known that Esty had suffered a miscarriage, and he would be tormented by a guilty conscience for the rest of his life. I told them that it depended on what Esty wanted and since she was still undecided, I was not yet prepared to withdraw my complaint, and that Davie should remain under arrest in the meantime.

The following morning, Esty told me to drop the charges, so I went to the police station to do so. I told my in-laws that I never, ever wanted to set my eyes on Davie again, no matter how remorseful he was.

Rabbi Walder, this is our story. Because of someone's senseless stupidity, we sit at home sad and alone thinking of what happiness we could have had. Davie has grown up very suddenly and is full of remorse and regret over how his foolishness ruined his sister's life — and his own. Maybe time will heal our wounds and I will eventually forgive Davie, but I don't think I will ever again be capable of meeting him face-to-face.

Tough Cop

D ear Rabbi Walder,
When I heard your story last week about the person whose driver's license was revoked, I began to think about a story that I was personally involved in. I am a policeman in the Northern Division of the Traffic Police, and I'm a tough cop who doesn't let drivers off the hook when they commit traffic offenses.

Every day we focus on one particular aspect of the law, and I try to carry out my tasks to the best of my ability. One day we might stop drivers who exceed the speed limit. Another day we check trucks for excess loads. On other days we do spot checks on licenses.

People think that getting caught for speeding is a matter of luck, but in my experience, a reckless driver who habitually drives at 90 mph will eventually get caught. It's not luck, but probability.

There's one thing which I do think is a matter of luck, though, and that's the nature of the policeman who catches you. Some cops are really soft at heart. They'll pull you over, and almost apologize for having stopped you, and give you a long explanation of which specific law you violated. The driver will probably grab the opportunity to have a friendly chat with the policeman, who feels guilty about handing out a fine in the first place. But others are quite the opposite — like me. We are stern-faced and not interested in hearing what the driver has to say. We simply write out the ticket and hand it to the driver before he has a chance to start "explaining."

Of course there are all kinds of drivers too. There's the kind who, when stopped for reckless driving, will invariably start whining and telling you his tragic life history. He'll tearfully tell you how nothing has ever gone right for him and that the whole world is against him. He'll really tug at your heartstrings and lots of policemen aren't able to withstand this — after all, everyone has an innate sense of mercy and wants to be kind. The tear-jerker can get away with a lot.

Most drivers have a basic sense of self-respect, though. They may ask to be let off, but they aren't willing to debase themselves. The easiest kind of driver is the one who quietly pulls over to the curb, hands over his papers, accepts his fine without a show of emotion, gives a quick nod and says, "Thank you." Although he drives off with a fine, his self-respect remains intact.

The most infuriating kind is the one who tries to insult the policeman and treat him like a speck of dirt. This driver will provoke you to fine him for additional offenses by making sarcastic comments like, "Look, officer, can't you see my front headlight is slightly cracked? You'd better write me another ticket, if you know how to write, that is." You don't have any option then but to write the ticket, knowing full well that Daddy is rich and is always there to take care of such matters.

Rabbi Walder, as an experienced traffic policeman, I consider myself to be above all this. I try never to take notice of the driver's behavior and I always write out the ticket, regardless of whether he's taunting me or crying his eyes out. Emotions have never played a role in my work. I've always given advice to my "softhearted" colleagues, telling them to have the courage to write out a ticket for the "crybabies." I tell them what a metamorphosis will take place when they do that! The "nebbich" suddenly becomes aggressive and nasty.

You learn a lot about human nature in this kind of work. Including your own — which brings me to my story.

Two years ago I took part in a special operation to man a roadblock at the Golani intersection, one of the main junctions in northern Israel, near Tiberias. Our instructions were officially classified as being "security/criminal" which meant in practice that we were out to catch criminals who were smuggling drugs over the Lebanese border into Israel. I stood at the roadblock and had to decide which cars would drive on freely and which would be flagged down by me. Certain cars invariably get stopped, because they simply "look suspicious." I can't give you any details.

Late one Thursday night, after about two hours on the job, I was feeling pretty bored when I spotted a battered Peugeot van, a car favored by Israeli Arabs. I stopped the car. As it came to a halt, I saw that the rear of the car was sunken with a heavy load, almost touching the ground in fact. Alarm bells went off in my head, and I knew I was onto something at last.

The driver got out of his battered car, looking nervous. To my surprise he was not an Arab, but a religious Jew with a beard and *peyos*! All his licenses were in order, and Mr. Joel Friedman was obviously not a terrorist or a drug smuggler. Still, I could tell by the look on his face that something was not right. He kept on glancing nervously at the back of the car and I realized that I was right to be suspicious. I handed him back his papers and he got into the car and prepared to drive off.

"Not so fast, Mr. Friedman," I said. "I want to check the rear of your van."

"Please," he stammered, "I'm in a rush to get home. It's very late."

"Just open the rear door," I replied in my sternest voice.

The walk from the driver's seat to the rear of the van seemed to take him forever. Now we in the police force know that a person's gait and facial expression are give-away signs and these have given away even the most experienced "actors." Watching him make his way to the back of the van, I was more certain than ever that Mr. Friedman had something to hide. When he finally reached the back door, he stood there staring at it. I shouted at him to open the door already.

With a sigh, he did so.

The sight that met my eyes was totally unexpected.

I found myself staring at a heap of dusty, uniformed soldiers, lying on top of each other — sound asleep! I listened to the chorus of gentle snoring, and said a silent prayer of thanks that they were all alive and well, just utterly exhausted.

Rabbi Walder, you realize that this story took place while the Israeli army was stationed in Southern Lebanon to protect Israel's northern border. There was constant guerrilla warfare with a large number of Israeli casualties. Every mother and father prayed for their son's safety and was relieved when he came home on leave safe and sound.

I put on my stern face again. "Mr. Friedman, now you are in real trouble — get all those soldiers out of your van, immediately!"

"Officer, if you want them out, you'll have to do it yourself," Mr. Friedman replied quietly. "These soldiers are exhausted — look at them! They're coming straight from the front. If you have the heart to wake them up, go ahead. I can't."

"No problem, Friedman, and don't think your *chutzpah* will get you anywhere."

I then shone my flashlight at the sleeping soldiers and shouted at them to get up. At first there was no reaction, and then a few of them stirred or blinked in their sleep, but nothing seemed to disturb them. So I climbed into the van and began to haul them out, one by one. They stumbled over to the side of the road, lay down, and continued sleeping!

Mr. Friedman looked on silently, but the look on his face said everything. I was sure he was thinking, "Aren't you ashamed of yourself, you heartless policeman?"

I addressed him in my most serious voice: "I am an officer of the law, and I will not tolerate any of this."

Once the van was empty I did a head count of the soldiers and I was amazed to discover that no less than fourteen soldiers had been loaded in. My first thought was that this would qualify to be in the Guinness Book of World Records!

"Mr. Friedman, I am going to fine you for a total of three traffic violations, and your driving license will be revoked for having taken fourteen passengers in your van."

To my surprise, he didn't seem to be the least concerned. He was only concerned about "his" sleeping soldiers.

"Look at them, sleeping like babies at the side of the road! Is your heart made of stone? Just think of their parents waiting anxiously for them to come home."

Now Mr. Friedman was really starting to get on my nerves. I considered arresting him for obstructing justice and insulting a policeman. Before I could say anything, a couple of the soldiers woke up, shot me dirty looks, and told me to leave Mr. Friedman alone. "He's doing us a great favor," they said. "Do you want to punish him for that and then abandon us here at the side of the road?" Their faces looked very young at that moment.

I don't know what got into me — maybe I was always so tough and hard, I don't know — but I told them that was exactly what I intended to do, and then I instructed Mr. Friedman to follow me to the nearest police station to take care of his license. I remained deaf to the soldiers' pleas.

At that moment my cellphone rang. It was my wife Ruth on the line. I know her well enough to know that she never calls me that late at night unless there is a very valid reason.

"What's the matter, Ruthie?"

She said one word: "Michael."

I felt faint. Our son Michael was serving in Lebanon.

"What?" My heart skipped a beat. " What happened to Michael?"

"He was released for the weekend, and he's not home yet. I'm getting nervous."

"What time was he released?"

"I don't know. He called me to say he was hitchhiking home. He was so tired he could hardly talk. He just told me that he was getting a ride in some battered, old van with a group of soldiers, and then the line went dead. I don't even know where he was when he called. It's the middle of the night, and I'm terrified."

I had to sit down on the street myself. "Don't worry, Ruthie dear," I said confidently. "I'm sure everything is fine. He's probably sound asleep. I...uh...may be able to check...don't ask me how...I'll call you right back..."

I walked over to the sleeping soldiers and took a close look at their faces. In no time I identified my beloved Michael sound asleep at the side of the road. With great difficulty, I managed to wake him and when he recognized me he started to blurt out "Abba," but I quickly hushed him because I was so ashamed.

"Michael, gather five of your comrades-in-arms and get into my police car! Just don't tell anyone that I'm your father."

I then called Mr. Friedman over and told him he could drive home with the remaining eight soldiers.

He stared at me. "And the fine?" he asked.

I did not reply.

"I *knew* you had a heart!" he exclaimed.

I felt myself blushing, and fortunately it was too dark to

notice. I was consumed with guilt and burning with shame. I had a heart? I had almost abandoned my beloved son, and thirteen other beloved sons, at the roadside. And there were no buses at that hour.

"Officer, are you going to let me off?" he persisted.

"Yes, Mr. Friedman, I am letting you off. But only because... because I was thinking of the soldiers' mothers..."

Suspicion

Dear Rabbi Walder,
I have two reasons for writing you this story — first, I feel a great need to unburden myself and tell someone about the pain I've been living with for the last six years, and second, I am sure my story can help others.

About six years ago, our oldest son went through a very difficult period. He was a teenager at the time and a student at a very well-known yeshivah. He couldn't deal well with the pressures he felt, and his studies deteriorated. Then he started hanging around with questionable characters.

At home, we repeatedly warned him to stay away from his new "friends" but he wouldn't listen to us — he was always sure that he knew better. This caused us a lot of heartache, but together with our criticism, we tried to show him our love and warmth, hoping that he would not "stray from the path" too far.

My husband told him, "Moishie, I understand that you are going through a difficult phase, and you certainly know that I think you are doing lots of foolish things. But I want you to listen to me now — I ask one thing of you: Don't do anything that might have permanent and serious consequences. There has to be a red line you must never, ever cross."

Moishie acted as if he wasn't listening to his father, and the situation continued to deteriorate.

One day someone called us and asked us to come to a meeting with some community leaders. We were very apprehensive — for good reason, it turned out. When we arrived, we were told that Moishie had been harassing a certain family for the last year. The details were terrible.

You can imagine how shocked we were. The deeds Moishie was accused of were so heinous that we were embarrassed to face these people. My husband was the first to recover from the shock, and he asked how they had tracked Moishie down. One of the men showed us a printout of calls made from Moishie's cellphone (we'd had no idea that he owned one). He went on to tell us that they'd been trying to track down the caller for more than six months, that the police had not taken the matter seriously, and that finally they had found a way to discover the phone number and thus they were led to Moishie.

I was so overcome with distress and shame that I couldn't speak — I could only cry. My husband asked what we should do now, and they said we should get Moishie to admit his guilt and sign a statement that he would never repeat these deeds. If he refused to sign, a complaint would be filed with the police.

When we got home, we immediately called Moishie into the living room for a discussion. He was in a very gloomy mood and denied any involvement in the affair. Naturally we didn't believe him. When we showed him a copy of the phone printout, he admitted that it was indeed his cellphone number but he once again vigorously denied any involvement. We could not believe him, and we told him so. We pointed out that he had even kept secret the fact that he had a cellphone.

All Moishie would say is, "I will not admit doing something that I never did."

"Moishie," we pleaded, "we realize you are ashamed to

admit your guilt to us, but you're only going to get into deeper trouble if the police get involved. Don't be so stubborn — just admit it."

He would not budge. In tears, I begged him to sign the statement that he would not repeat his deeds.

"Mom, I have no problem signing a statement that I won't do anything like this, but I refuse to sign anything stating that I did these things. I didn't make those phone calls."

The police were called, and Moishie was summoned for questioning. The policemen questioned him in our presence. Once again he denied his involvement. They turned to us: "Your son apparently likes getting himself into trouble. If he admits his guilt, he'll get off the hook lightly. The proof is irrefutable. Why is he being so stubborn?" To make a long and painful story short, Rabbi Walder, Moishie was found guilty and put on probation.

We were all shattered. Moishie left yeshivah and became irreligious. He spent several years "on the streets," and then gradually started making his way back to a Jewish life. He married a girl who helped him a lot. We assisted with the wedding and the setting up of their home. We felt it was our duty as parents, no matter how far away from our way of life he was, but deep down we were in pain. Our relationship had never returned to what it was before the whole affair.

A short time ago I was talking to a good friend and by "chance" (I know that there is no such thing as "chance" in this world) she told me the story of a wealthy, prominent family in our city. About ten years ago, it was discovered that money was disappearing from their home and the chief suspect was their cleaning lady.

The family hired a private detective, who placed a bag of money in their house. He told the family to call him when the woman left the house. As soon as she left, it was discovered that the money had disappeared, and the detective rushed to the bus stop where the woman was waiting. He told her he was sent by the family and demanded she open her purse. She did so and of course the bag was there.

The police opened an investigation. The woman maintained her innocence. Her husband and father begged the family to drop charges, but they insisted that a thief must pay. The woman was convicted. Her good name was destroyed, her husband almost divorced her, and even her own family members were careful not to leave money lying around the house. The woman's life was ruined.

One day, her former boss — the woman of the family for whom she had worked — called her with astonishing information. The family had very good reason to believe that she was not in fact the thief, they said, and they wished to ask her forgiveness. They wanted to pay her compensation for wrongfully accusing her. Later, when they met together, they pressed her to accept their apology and generous financial compensation.

She replied, "You ruined my life. No amount of financial compensation can restore my good name."

The family appealed to the courts to re-open the case. This took time, and after several years of appeals, the case finally reached the Israeli High Court of Justice. The High Court agreed to re-open the investigation, and the police now turned their attention to the one person who seemed to have been forgotten in the first investigation — one of the family's sons, who had informed the private detective when the cleaning lady had left their home, and who had told the detective that the bag of money had disappeared. During this second police investigation, it became clear that he was the actual thief and it was he who had slipped the money into the woman's purse.

How did this truth finally come to light?

This wicked, corrupt person (you will shortly discover why I use these adjectives) continued with his evil deeds. Money continued to disappear from the house but now they could not accuse their cleaning lady. It never occurred to them that their own son, who was a respected figure in the community, was the thief. The truth was eventually revealed when his involvement in another dishonest affair came to light. Overnight all his evil deeds were discovered. He discarded his religious "disguise" and the family had to acknowledge what had been going under their nose for several years. That was when they immediately called their former cleaning lady.

Rabbi Walder, you must be wondering what this family has to do with my story. I'm getting to that. Well, when my friend told me this story, the name of the family rang a bell. I made one call to my husband at work and he confirmed my suspicions. The man who had done such evil was none other than the man who had confronted us with evidence of our Moishie's crime! It was he who had pressured Moishie to admit his guilt, and it was he who had called the police.

Our inquiries confirmed what was by then beginning to become obvious: *he* was the one who had been harassing the family, not our Moishie. He had gone into Moishie's room at the yeshivah and made his harassing calls from Moishie's cellphone, while Moishie was in the *beis midrash*. When he finished the call, he simply put the cellphone back in Moishie's cupboard and left the building. This was a man who had falsely accused many innocent and unsuspecting people. He himself had committed terrible deeds and he had tried to cover himself by committing even more terrible deeds. This was his mode of action, and he caused many families to distrust their own children. It makes me shudder to think of the damage that he wrought.

As soon as we discovered the truth, we called our Moishie to our house and told him what we had learned. We wept and begged him to forgive us. He accepted our apologies, but he must surely feel that nothing can restore the lost years, the hurt, the shame, the terrible feeling of being accused of a crime when you know you are innocent and no one believes you.

I promised Moishie that for the rest of my life I would try to compensate him for what I did, for having falsely accused him and for not standing by him when he desperately needed us.

Love Thy Neighbor

ear Rabbi Walder,
About fifteen years ago, when I was twelve years old, my parents got into a bitter dispute with our neighbors. We lived across from each other on the top floor of our apartment building.

They (the W. family) began to enlarge their apartment by breaking through to the roof and building a partial second story. We also intended to do this in the future. However, the size of their extension exceeded what was allowed in their building permit, and my parents discovered, as the extension was nearing completion, that the neighbors had built into some of "our" space.

My parents summoned the neighbors to appear before a *Beis Din* but they refused to come — I don't know why. The *Beis Din* issued a statement stating that the neighbors were in contempt of the *Beis Din*, which caused them much embarrassment in the community. My parents were also granted permission by the *Beis Din* to sue their neighbors in the civil courts. The judges in the civil case ruled in my parents' favor and ordered the W. family to pay my parents several thousand dollars in damages or demolish the extension. They decided to pay my parents. However, they were unable to pay the full amount at that time. My parents decided to call in debt collectors who burst into the neighbors' apartment and tried to confiscate their possessions. Influential people in our community tried to talk my parents into being more flexible and understanding, but my parents refused to budge, and they insisted on being paid immediately — up to the last cent.

I was a young boy at the time, as I said, and was so caught up in this dispute that whenever I saw any of the W. children, I would start up a fight with them. I'm embarrassed to write this now, but the dispute between the two families grew to such proportions that it split the entire neighborhood into two camps. Both children and adults took sides in the dispute!

Legally my family had won the case and we received the whole amount of the compensation down to the very last cent. However, it was a hollow victory which left a deep hatred between the two families. This hatred hung like a heavy cloud over us, over the whole building, and over the entire neighborhood.

The burning animosity was fueled daily. If I opened the front door at the same time as one of the neighbors did, I could literally feel his hatred towards me. We lived in an intolerable situation of tension and nerves. Matters did not improve over the years — they only got worse.

When I was in high school, and later in yeshivah, word of the family feud got around and it was not very easy for me. However, that was just a warm-up for what was awaiting me when I entered the *shidduch* scene.

What can I tell you? No *shadchanim* came knocking on our door with offers. It soon became clear that when a prospective *shidduch* started making inquiries about me and my family, they soon got to hear about the feud, and they quickly dropped the suggestion. Nobody wanted to marry into a family of "trouble-makers." It didn't matter who was in the right. And from the point of view of the W. family, we were the villains. They told people how we had chased them mercilessly through the courts until they went into debt to pay us, etc., etc. Nobody cared that the *dayanim* had condemned their behavior in the strongest possible terms, and that they were found to be the guilty party.

Anyway, eventually I realized that not one of the W. children, nor any of us, ever got to go out on a *shidduch* date!

One by one, all my friends got married and I was left waiting for a *shadchan* to come with a suggestion for me. Around that time one of the other neighbors told my mother that the W. family's biggest fear was that I would get married before their oldest daughter Chava! I was shocked at the extent of the hatred that this revealed, but the more I thought about it, I realized that my parents felt exactly the same way at the thought of Chava getting married before me!

My father by this time had become a bitter man, old before his time. Lines of suffering marked his face. I understood what he must be feeling at the sight of his children reaching marriageable age and being prevented from setting up a home. He saw the neighbors as a cruel enemy trying to ruin our lives and deprive us of the chance for happiness.

Two years ago, I turned twenty-five. I was the oldest child in my family and I had three younger brothers and one younger sister who were all of marriageable age. We were all at home waiting in vain for a *shidduch*! I became quite alarmed by this situation and realized that if I didn't do something to change matters we were all doomed to stay in that apartment with our bitter parents and all the tension and our "wonderful neighbors" for the rest of our lives.

I had become quite friendly with Chezky, a young man of my age who had already made a name for himself as a successful *shadchan*. Chezky worked very hard to arrange *shidduchim* for me, and my parents left it up to me to make the necessary inquiries. They trusted me; after all, I was no longer a youngster.

Chezky and I quickly became close friends. He was the same age as I, and he had been married for four years and had three young children. Shortly after we met, Chezky sized up my predicament and told me that things did not look very optimistic for my siblings and me because our family's name was really besmirched. I spent many hours talking to Chezky trying to find a solution to the predicament. I told him that as far as I was concerned, I was prepared to repay the neighbors the full amount of the damages they had paid us, if they would leave us alone and stop giving us such a bad name. (This was a major concession on my part, as I had grown up hating them. However, I was determined not to let the family feud continue into the next generation.) Unfortunately, neither Chezky nor I seriously thought that it was practical.

One day, Chezky called me and said, "Listen, you'll never guess who called and asked me to find a *shidduch* for his children — your neighbor!"

I fully understood the situation Mr. W. was in — he had several sons and daughters of marriageable age and he had been unable to find a *shidduch* for any of them for the very same reason that my siblings and I were still single. I suggested that Chezky try to hint at making peace between the two warring families. He tried, but the man was as stubborn and bitter as my father, and would not listen. Chezky told me that his wife was quite friendly with the oldest daughter, Chava. Maybe she would be able to talk with Chava and through her get her father to soften up.

Chezky's wife was soon able to report that Chava was as fed up by this terrible feud that was ruining her family as I was. It seemed that the anger and pain that had become a part of our home was also felt in their family.

I devised a plan of action. I asked Chezky to ask his wife to ask Chava to approach her parents and delicately mention that we were prepared to speak to them about the money. Chava did so, and reported back that it was a waste of time. Her parents would not hear of having anything to do with us. Chezky and his wife told me (and I suppose they told Chava too) that if it were up to her and me, then it would be possible to end this terrible feud, but unfortunately it was not just up to the two of us.

At home I tried to reason with my parents and tell them that it would be a terrible tragedy if none of their children were able to find a *shidduch* because of their quarrel with the neighbors. Chezky told me that Chava tried to reason with her parents along the same lines, but neither of us had any success.

One day I was talking to Chezky on the phone, trying to work out details of a new plan I had about making peace between the two families. It was very complicated trying to work out details of this plan, with Chezky and his wife acting as messengers who passed on my ideas to Chava, so Chezky suggested that we put Chava on the line and have a conference call. During the call, I presented my plan to Chava, and she added her comments, as did Chezky and his wife, and we all tried to work out the finer details of my plan. At the end of the call, I suggested that we both check out certain aspects of the plan and report back to Chezky in a few days.

Chezky had another suggestion: that Chava report back directly to me, in order to save time. When the conference call ended, I immediately called Chezky back. "Chezky, don't even think in the direction you are thinking."

"I'm not thinking of anything in particular at all — I just want to shorten the chain of communication."

I didn't believe that Chezky was being so naive, but it didn't matter anyhow, for I knew there was no chance.

Chava did indeed report back to me, and initially our conversations were very businesslike. Then the conversations became more personal, and we realized we had a lot in common, besides the feud. Things were indeed moving in a certain direction, and I informed my parents that I had received a certain suggestion for a *shidduch* and I did not want them to interfere. My parents were surprised and happily agreed — after all, I was already twenty-five years old, and they knew that this *shidduch* had come through the trustworthy Chezky.

Chava and I eventually came to the realization that although we were very compatible, we would never be able to get married because of the family feud. Since there was nothing else to say, we broke off all contact. After a week of suffering, I called Chezky and asked him to find out how Chava was doing. It took him just a few minutes to call me back to tell me that Chava was suffering too and wanted to know how I was doing. Once I heard that, I immediately asked him to speak to her parents and mine and make the suggestion official.

Chezky spoke to Chava, and she agreed to my suggestion but she sent back a message asking if I was aware of the earthquake this suggestion would cause. I replied in the affirmative.

Sure enough, when Chezky suggested the *shidduch* to both sets of parents, the anger and shock were very deep. As if they had coordinated their reactions beforehand, Chava's father told her, and my father informed me, that if we wanted to get married it would be "on the street" — that is, with no help from them. We each replied to our parents separately: So be it!

Chezky suggested that each family consult their own Rav for advice. They did so and, within a week, both sets of parents relented. It took another two weeks to arrange the actual engagement and to get the two sides to formally meet. Many of my parents' friends helped arrange the meeting and in the end the engagement party was set for a Saturday night.

Words cannot describe how many tears were shed at that *Melaveh Malkah* celebration. My family, Chava's family, all the residents of our apartment building, and many of our mutual friends and neighbors all cried about how much had been lost over the years with the quarrel between the two families. But they were tears of great joy as well, and of gratitude to Hashem for our *shidduch* and for the reconciliation between the families.

Our engagement was also the turning point in the good fortune of both families. Within a year, two of my siblings and three of Chava's got engaged.

Rabbi Walder, I am writing you this story with my dear wife Chava's total agreement. We want all your listeners who might have a disagreement with one of their neighbors to hear our story and take our advice. Don't stand on your *kavod*, it is sometimes worth giving in in order to avoid a battle which will eat away at your soul and your happiness.

Chava and I are very happily married, *baruch Hashem*. We live in an apartment building with twelve other families. When we hear the slightest hint of any disagreement between neighbors, Chava gives me a very meaningful look, and I know just what she is thinking about: the whole story I have just written to you, and much more than that.

Glossary

The following glossary provides a partial explanation of some of the Hebrew, Yiddish (Y.), and Aramaic (A.) words and phrases used in this book. The spellings and explanations reflect the way the specific word is used herein. Often, there are alternate spellings and meanings for the words.

AD ME'AH V'ESRIM: "until 120," a traditional birthday blessing.

BA'AL TESHUVAH: a formerly non-observant Jew who has returned to Jewish tradition and practice.

BACHUR: a young man; a yeshivah student.

BARUCH HASHEM: "Thank God!"

BASHERT: (Y.) one's intended mate.

BEIS DIN: a rabbinical court of law.

BEIS MIDRASH: the study hall of a yeshivah.

BITACHON: faith and trust in God.

CHASAN: a bridegroom.

CHAVRUSA: (A.) a Torah study partner.

CHEDER: (Y.) a Jewish primary school for boys.

CHIZUK: strengthening and encouragement.

CHOL HAMO'ED: the intermediate days of the Festivals.

CHUPPAH: a wedding canopy; a wedding.

CHUTZPAH: (Y.) nerve; brashness.

DA'AS TORAH: the accepted, Torah-based opinions of recognized rabbinic authorities.

DAYAN: a rabbinical judge.

EISHES CHAYIL: a "woman of valor," from *Mishlei* 31:10–31.

GET: a Jewish bill of divorce.

KADDISH: a prayer sanctifying God's name; the mourner's prayer.

KAVOD: honor; dignity.

KOLLEL: a center for advanced Torah study for adult students, mostly married men.

LEVAYAH: a funeral.

MAZAL: fate; one's determined fortune.

MENTSCH: (Y.) lit., "a man," i.e., a decent person.

MEZUZAH: a rolled parchment containing the prayer *Shema Yisrael*, placed on doorposts in Jewish homes.

MINYAN: a quorum of ten Jewish men, obligatory for congregational prayer.

MISHLEI: the Book of Proverbs.

MOSHAV: an agricultural settlement.

NACHAS: (Y.) satisfaction.

PEYOS: sidelocks.

ROSH YESHIVAH: the dean of a Torah Academy.

SECHACH: the roof of the sukkah, usually made from branches and leaves.

SHADCHAN: a matchmaker.

SHEVA BERACHOS: the seven blessings recited at a wedding; any of the festive meals held in honor of the bride and groom during the week following the wedding, at which the seven blessings are recited.

SHIDDUCH: a marital match.

SHIUR: a Torah lesson.

SHIVAH: the seven-day period of mourning.

SIMCHAH: joy; a joyous occasion.

SUKKAH: a temporary booth in which Jews live during Sukkos.

TEFILLAH: prayer.

TEHILLIM: the Book of Psalms.

TESHUVAH: repentance.

TZA'AR GIDUL BANIM: the pain of raising children.

TZADDIK / TZADEKES: a pious, righteous man/woman.

YAHRTZEIT: (Y.) the anniversary of a death.

YESHIVAH BACHUR: a yeshivah student.

YIDDISHKEIT: (Y.) Judaism.